Claudia and Mean Janine

**Look for these and other books
in the Baby-sitters Club series:**

Claudia and Mean Janine

Ann M. Martin

AN
APPLE
PAPERBACK

SCHOLASTIC INC.
New York Toronto London Auckland Sydney

ISBN 0-590-41041-5

12 11 10 9 8 7 6 5 4 3 2   7 8 9/8 0 1 2/9

Printed in the U.S.A.   28

First Scholastic printing, September 1987

*For
Aunt Adele
and
Uncle Paul*

*The author would like to thank
Dr. Claudia Werner
for her sensitive evaluation
of the manuscript.*

CHAPTER 1

"Coffee's ready!"

"Where's my sweater?"

"Mom! I ironed my blouse last night and now it's wrinkled! How did that happen?"

"I need two dollars!"

"I *said*, the *coffee* is *ready!*"

It was a pretty typical morning at my house. Summer or winter, my parents and sister and I are always rushing off in different directions. Since it was July and school was out, my sister Janine was off to advanced summer courses at Stoneybrook University, I was off to a drawing class, and Mom and Dad were just off to work as usual. The only one who wasn't off to any place was Mimi, my grandmother.

On school mornings, I wake up slowly. Mimi has to prod me to get out of bed, prod me to get dressed, prod me to eat breakfast, and prod me to go out the front door. This is because I don't like school.

In the summer, no one has to prod me. I like vacation and I *love* art classes. I love drawing and painting and crafts.

I am thirteen years old, which means I am now officially a teenager. Mom says that doesn't mean much, because I've always been a teenager. By that, I think she means that I can be difficult to live with. I'm smart, but I don't like school or homework. My family is conservative, but I'm wild. I like loud clothes. I like to dance. I can be a real pain sometimes.

On the other hand, Janine, who is sixteen, has never been a teenager, according to my mother. Janine is smart and likes school. Actually, that's not quite right. She's super-smart (a genius), and she doesn't just go to school. She goes, as I mentioned, to college. Well, she takes college courses, but she's still a high school student. She'll be a junior at Stoneybrook High this fall. Anyway, she never gives anybody a lick of trouble. She studies, studies, studies. My parents think she's wonderful. They brag to our relatives about how she's only sixteen and can handle college work. They expect her to become something really important like a physicist.

Janine wears clothes that are blah, blah, blah. When she outgrows them and passes them along to me, I pass them right along to Kristy

2

Thomas or Mary Anne Spier, who live across the street. They don't care too much about clothes, but I wouldn't be caught dead in Janine's things. I'd rather have to pay for all new clothes with the money I earn baby-sitting than wear Janine's free but yucky button-down shirts, gray kilts, and crew-neck sweaters.

Do you get the feeling that Janine and I are different from each other?

To be frank, my sister and I have next to nothing in common. I'm outgoing and have a lot of friends; Janine sticks to herself and has almost no friends. (That's what happens when your parents want you to be a physicist.) I've already had two semi-boyfriends; Janine, quite possibly, doesn't know what boys are. I have lots of interests: reading mysteries, baby-sitting, painting, and drawing; all Janine cares about is her computer.

I can hardly even talk to Janine. She uses such big words, it's like talking to *Webster's Dictionary*. Sometimes she teases me about not being as smart as she is. Mom says she does that because underneath, she wishes she were a little like me, with friends and interests and stuff, and feels left out of our family. Mom also says that I'm not fair to Janine sometimes — that inside, Janine is sensitive and loving, and creative in her own way, but that

3

I don't see those things because I won't look beyond the big words. Also, I wouldn't admit this to just anybody, but I have a feeling I'm a big disappointment to my parents. Brains are important to them, and I want to be an artist, not a scientist. I've tried to tell them you have to be smart to be a good artist, but they're not convinced. So, okay, I'm a teeny weeny bit jealous of my sister. She can *always* make our parents happy.

Anyway, on that busy Wednesday morning, I finished dressing in my favorite art class outfit — black jeans, a giant bright blue T-shirt, and a snake bracelet that I wore above my elbow — and ran downstairs. I was the second one into the kitchen.

Mimi greeted me in her gentle way. "Good morning, my Claudia," she said softly. I hardly notice Mimi's accent anymore, but she does have one. Our family is Japanese, and Mimi, who is Mom's mother, didn't come to the United States until she was in her thirties. I'm surprised she speaks English as well as she does, I mean, considering that for half her life she spoke only Japanese.

"Morning, Mimi!" I replied.

Mimi was fixing breakfast. (She was not, however, the person who'd been yelling about the coffee earlier. That was my father. Every morning, he comes downstairs as soon as he stumbles out of bed, and gets the coffee going pronto for himself and Mom. They practically can't see without a little caffeine in their bodies. Mimi and I drink herbal tea.)

I sat down at my place at the kitchen table. A few moments later, Mom joined me, then Janine, and then my father. Mimi served up the scrambled eggs she'd made, and sat down next to me.

"This is lovely, Mother," said my mom to Mimi. "Honestly, I don't know what we'd do without you."

"Me, neither!" I added.

"And I do not know what I would do if I did not have you to take care of," said Mimi earnestly.

Mimi has been living with us since before I was born. My grandfather, Mimi's husband, died not long after my mom and dad got married.

"And what is everybody going to do today?" asked Mimi.

"The usual," replied my father cheerfully. "Oh, but I'll be a little late tonight," he added. "We have a five-thirty meeting this afternoon. It may go on for a while." Dad is a partner in an investment business in Stamford, Connecticut, which is not far from Stoneybrook.

"The usual for me, too," said Mom. Mom is the head librarian at the local public library. This has been a big boon to Janine, who needs books the way most people need food and water. It has not been much help to me, since the only books I read are mysteries. My favorites are Nancy Drews, which the library doesn't have, and which I have to hide from my parents. They think Nancy Drews aren't worthwhile.

"I," said Janine, "have one class this morning and two this afternoon. I believe I'll spend the day on campus. I can work at the computer library between classes."

"What a thrill," I murmured. Janine tried to make everything she did sound important and wonderful.

"Claudia," warned my mother.

Janine looked hurt. "Well, what are *you* going to do today?" she asked me. "Reinvent the wheel?"

"Ha, ha." Janine can't even make a joke. "No," I said. "I'm going to drawing class this morning. After lunch I'm going to baby-sit for Jamie Newton for a couple of hours. Then Stacey and I are going shopping, and then I have a meeting of the Baby-sitters Club."

"Oh," said Janine in a small voice. She looked a little wistful.

The Baby-sitters Club is something Kristy Thomas (from across the street) thought up. She and I and three other girls have this club that is really a business. Kristy is our president. We earn money baby-sitting for the families in our neighborhood. Three afternoons a week we hold half-hour meetings in my bedroom. (I have a phone.) Our clients call us during those times to tell us when they need baby-sitters. Then Mary Anne Spier checks the calendar in our Baby-sitters Club Record Book to see who's available, and we call the parent back to say which one of us will be sitting. The parents like this arrangement because they only have to make one phone call to reach five girls, so they're pretty much guaranteed a sitter. It saves them time.

I'm the vice-president of the club.

Mary Anne is the secretary. She's in charge of our record book, where we keep track of our clients, their addresses and phone numbers, our appointments, and stuff like that. Mary Anne is perfect for the job. She's well-organized and smart, and she has the neatest handwriting of anyone in the club. I've lived across the street from Mary Anne for as long as I can remember, and although I like her, I still feel I don't know her very well. Mary Anne's on the shy side, and she and Kristy have always been best friends.

Our club treasurer is Stacey McGill. She keeps track of the money we make. Stacey moved to Stoneybrook about a year ago, and she and I got to be really good friends. We're very much alike. Stacey's from New York, where it's okay to be wild. I don't think anyone from New York could ever be blah.

Then there's Dawn Schafer. Dawn joined the Baby-sitters Club a few months after Kristy, Mary Anne, Stacey, and I started it. She's also a newcomer to Connecticut. She and her mom and brother moved here from California after her parents got divorced. (Her mom grew up in Stoneybrook.) Dawn and Mary Anne quickly became good friends, and Mary Anne was the one who got Dawn into the club.

For the longest time, Dawn wasn't an officer of the club because the rest of us were filling the four main posts. Then Kristy made her the official alternate officer, which means that she can take over for anyone who has to miss a meeting.

At first, Kristy was pretty jealous of the friendship between Mary Anne and Dawn, but she likes Dawn all right now. Besides, Kristy's had plenty to think about. Our club president

8

was just in a wedding — her own mother's! Kristy's parents got divorced several years ago, and Kristy and her mom, her two big brothers Sam and Charlie, and her little brother David Michael had done okay on their own. But when Mrs. Thomas met this man, Watson Brewer, the two of them fell in love and finally got married. Kristy was the bridesmaid.

I went to the wedding. It was wonderful. Kristy wore a long dress, and shoes with heels, and flowers in her hair. It was very romantic. The one bad thing about the marriage is that the Thomases have to move. They're not going far — just into Watson's house, which is across town — but it will cause some problems for the Baby-sitters Club. For instance, Kristy has to travel three miles to get to our meetings. We're hoping her brother Charlie will be able to drive her, even if we have to pay him.

I was shaken out of my daydreaming by the sound of dishes clattering in the sink. Breakfast was over. Mom and Dad were clearing the table. Janine was swallowing the last of her orange juice. Quickly, I finished my scrambled eggs.

"So," said Janine, out of the blue, "may I ask how your agency plans to function once your founder is residing in a different district?"

9

"You may," I replied, stalling. I had no idea what she was talking about.

"Oh, I understand," said Janine. "You want to play games. Well, I'll comply. All right, how *does* your agency plan to function once your founder is residing in a different district?"

"Huh?"

"I *said* — "

"Janine, talk in English, will you?"

"I *am!*" Janine looked hurt again. "I can't help it if this is the manner in which I speak."

"And I can't help it if I don't understand you."

"Oh, never mind," said Janine. She sighed. It might have been a sad sigh, it might have been an exasperated one. I couldn't tell. "I was simply trying to uphold my end of a meaningful conversation with my sibling."

"You were trying to *what?*"

"Talk to you!" exploded Janine.

"Well, why didn't you just say so?"

"I *did*." Janine stood up. "Very well. Have fun drawing and baby-sitting and shopping." How did Janine always manage to make me feel that I couldn't do anything worthwhile?

"And you have fun talking to machines!" I yelled after her as she left the kitchen.

Janine mumbled something that sounded

like, "At least they communicate with me." Now what was that supposed to mean?

It was another happy morning at the Kishis'.

As I left the house a little while later, Mimi put her arms around me and said, "Have fun today, my Claudia."

"I will," I replied, giving her a kiss.

Janine watched us from the front yard. Then she looked away. When her ride came along, she got into the car without even waving to us.

CHAPTER 2

I'm the first to admit it — I'm a junk food addict. I like candy. I like cookies. I like things with funny names such as Ho-Ho's, Ring Dings, Ding-Dongs, and Twinkies. I stock up on the stuff I like and stash it around my room. Since my Nancy Drew books are also hidden, I have to know a lot of good hiding places. If anyone were to search my room, they'd find cupcakes in the desk drawer, licorice in my pencil case, *The Clue of the Tapping Heels* and *The Message in the Hollow Oak* under my mattress, M&M's in my jewelry box, and *The Clue in the Crossword Cipher* at the bottom of a box of art supplies.

To get ready for our Baby-sitters Club meeting that day, I got out the M&M's. I also got a box of pretzels from the kitchen. They were for Stacey and Dawn. Stacey's diabetic and can't eat candy, and Dawn's into health food. I don't think pretzels are particularly healthy,

12

but I suppose they're better than M&M's. I also set out our record book, and another book that Kristy insists we keep up-to-date — our Baby-sitters Club Notebook, which is a sort of diary. We're supposed to record every single baby-sitting job in it, and then read it about once a week so we know what's going on at the homes where the other club members have baby-sat.

At five-fifteen, my friends started to show up. Stacey was first. She walked proudly into my room, looking smug.

"I didn't know you were going to get your hair cut!" I exclaimed when I saw her.

"I decided not to say anything," Stacey replied. "I wasn't sure how I'd look. Do you like it?"

"I love it! Did you get it permed again?"

"Yup. But after this I might let the perm grow out."

Stacey sat on my bed. Her blonde hair, which had been long and fluffy, was now cut to just above her shoulders. It made her look older.

"Gosh," I said, "maybe I should get my hair cut."

"Oh, don't!" cried Stacey. "Your hair is amazing. How long did it take you to grow it to that length?"

"Years," I admitted.

"It's so beautiful. Don't you dare touch it!"

"Touch what?" asked a voice. Dawn was standing in my doorway.

"Speaking of long hair . . ." said Stacey.

"Hi, you guys." Dawn came in and eased herself onto the floor. She had to swing her hair out before she sat down. That's how long *her* hair is. And it's white-blonde.

When Dawn and I stand next to each other, we look kind of like a photograph and its negative.

"Her hair," Stacey said, answering Dawn's question. "Just because I got mine cut, Claudia — "

"Aughh!" shrieked Dawn. "I didn't even notice. Oh, Stace, it looks fantastic!"

"Thanks," said Stacey, grinning.

A few moments later, Kristy and Mary Anne showed up. Mary Anne joined Dawn on the floor. We'd all been leaving my director's chair for Kristy. She likes to sit in it and take charge. Sometimes she wears a visor, or sticks a pencil over one ear. Anything to make her stand out as our president.

"Okay, baby-sitters," said Kristy, after she and Mary Anne had oohed and aahed over Stacey's haircut. "Business first. Stacey, what's in the treasury?"

Stacey had brought a rumpled manila en-

14

velope along with her. "Give me your dues first, you guys," she said.

We each forked over a dollar.

Stacey put the money on the bed and emptied the contents of the envelope over it. "Nineteen dollars even," she announced. She said this after one pretty quick glance at the bills and change, which is why she's our treasurer.

"Not bad," said Kristy. "Well, I have two interesting pieces of news, speaking of the money. One is that Charlie passed his driver's test today."

"Yea!" cheered the rest of us.

"The other is that I asked him about driving me to the meetings and to sitting jobs in this neighborhood after we move to Watson's."

"Yes?" I said eagerly. The whole future of the club depended on whether Kristy could get to the meetings.

"I offered to pay him a dollar for each trip he had to make — that means two dollars for every meeting."

Mary Anne, Stacey, Dawn, and I were practically biting our nails. We had discussed the amount of Kristy's offer endlessly. Would Charlie laugh at a dollar? Would he even want the job of driving Kristy all over town? It was important to us because we had decided to pay

Charlie out of the club dues. We didn't think it was right to ask the president of her own club to pay for car rides when no one else had to.

"And," Kristy went on, "he said a dollar is too" — I groaned — "much!" she cried. "He said fifty cents each way is plenty!"

"All right!"

"So we don't have to worry. The problem is solved. And cheaply!"

The phone rang then, and I picked it up. "Hello. Baby-sitters Club."

"Hello, this is Dr. Johanssen."

"Oh, hi," I said. "It's Claudia."

"Oh, Claudia. I need a sitter for Friday evening next week. Mr. Johanssen and I are going to a cocktail party. We'll need someone from six until about eight."

"Okay, I'll call you right back."

I got off the phone. "That was Charlotte's mother," I told the members of the club. "She needs someone from six to eight, a week from Friday."

Mary Anne checked the calendar in the record book. "You and Stacey are free," she announced.

I looked at Stacey. "You go," I said. "Charlotte really likes you. You're her favorite sitter."

"Thanks," said Stacey. "That's great. I haven't seen her in a while."

I called Dr. Johanssen back to tell her that Stacey would be sitting. Then we took a few more phone calls.

When the phone finally stopped ringing, Kristy said, "You guys, I have an idea."

I raised an eyebrow. Kristy has more ideas than anyone I know.

"Yeah?" said Stacey, sounding slightly suspicious.

"See, I thought last week went pretty well," Kristy began.

Kristy was referring to the days before her mother's wedding when, believe it or not, the members of the Baby-sitters Club had taken care of fourteen children. What had happened was that all these friends and relatives of Kristy's mother and Watson Brewer had shown up to help them get ready for the wedding. Only they brought their kids along, since they were coming from out of town and were planning to stay until the wedding was over. Mrs. Thomas knew the kids would just be in the way while the adults were trying to cook and stuff, so the club members sat for all of them for five days straight at Kristy's house. It really had gone well. We were very proud of ourselves.

"*I* think we did a good job," I agreed cautiously.

"Well, I got to thinking," Kristy went on. "Here it is, summer vacation. We're out of school, the children we sit for are out of school, and at least until next month when two of us are going away, there isn't much to do around here. In other words, there are a lot of kids at loose ends."

"Yeah?" said Stacey for the second time. We all wanted Kristy to get to the point.

"So how about a play group?"

"A what?" asked Dawn.

"A play group," Kristy repeated. "Sort of like day camp, except shorter. We could easily run one this month. It'd be great for the kids."

"But when would we baby-sit?" asked Mary Anne.

"Oh, in the afternoons and evenings. And weekends," Kristy added. "We'd just hold the play group a few mornings a week. It could be outdoors, in somebody's yard, just like last week at my house. We could tell all our regular customers about it, and they could send their kids over any time they wanted. We could charge, say, three dollars per kid per morning. That's a bargain for our clients, and even divided five ways, the money should be good for us, since chances are there wouldn't be enough jobs for every single one of us to be sitting if we *weren't* holding the play group."

"It *would* be kind of fun," I said. "Just think, all the kids we sit for would get to know each other."

"Yes!" said Mary Anne. "We can ask Jamie Newton, the Pikes, Jenny Prezzioso. . . ."

"The Barrett kids," added Dawn.

"Nina and Eleanor Marshall," I suggested.

"Charlotte," Stacey offered.

Kristy's eyes were gleaming. She was glad we liked her idea. "As soon as we get it all worked out, we'll call our clients," she said excitedly.

"We can entertain the kids just the way we did last week," I pointed out. "Art projects, stories, games."

"Their parents will like that," said Kristy thoughtfully.

"Hey!" I exclaimed. "Remember when Jamie Newton had to spend one morning with all the kids last week? His mother said she thought it would be good for him because it would help him learn to get along with other children. Maybe other parents will like that, too."

"Good point," said Kristy. "Hey, Mary Anne, maybe you better take notes. We might want to remember this stuff."

Mary Anne began scribbling in the notebook.

"Where should we hold the play group?" Kristy asked. "We can't have it at my house.

We'll be moving soon. We better not have it at your house, either, Mary Anne, since your dad works. I think the parents would want to know that an adult was around."

"Good point," said Dawn. "I guess I'm out, then. Mom's still looking for a job. She could find one any day."

"I'd love to have it here," I said, "but I don't know. Mimi has seemed awfully tired lately."

"Is she all right?" asked Mary Anne quickly.

"Fine. She just lies down a lot."

"My house would be okay, I think," said Stacey. "And Mom is usually around. I'll have to check with her, but I'm sure it'll be all right."

"Stacey's house?" Kristy asked the rest of us.

We nodded.

Our newest business had a home.

CHAPTER 3

As soon as Mrs. McGill gave Stacey permission to use their house, my friends and I decided to spend one afternoon talking to our clients about the play group in person. We thought the door-to-door approach would be nicer than just a flier stuck in a mailbox, and nicer even than a phone call. So after lunch one day, the five of us set off.

We *did* have fliers with us. We had spent a long time writing the flier, making sure it included all the information parents would need to know. We planned to hand them out in person, though, and then stay around to answer questions.

This is what our flier looked like:

SUMMER PLAY GROUP

Give your kids a treat!
Art projects, stories, games!
Come to the Baby-sitters Club
Summer Play Group!

Place: *Stacey McGill's backyard*
612 Fawcett Avenue
Time: *9:00–12:30 — Mondays,*
Wednesdays, Fridays during July
Cost: *$3 per child per morning*

For further details, call:
THE BABY-SITTERS CLUB
KL 5-3231
Mondays, Wednesdays, Fridays, 5:30–6:00

SUMMER PLAY GROUP:
the unique alternative to baby-sitting.

Our first stop was Jamie Newton's house. We found four-year-old Jamie, his mom, and his baby sister, Lucy, in the front yard.

"Hi-hi!" called Jamie when he saw us. "Are you here to baby-sit me?"

"No," I said, laughing. "Five baby-sitters! What would you do with five baby-sitters, Jamie?"

"Have *lots* of fun," he replied cheerfully.

"Hi, Mrs. Newton," said Kristy. "Hiya, Lucy."

Lucy is only about seven months old. She's adorable. She can sit up, and she knows how to crawl. Not very fast yet, but she's getting there. She gave us a big grin, and we could see that a couple of new teeth were coming in.

Lucy was sitting on a blanket next to Mrs. Newton, teething on a cookie and playing with a colorful set of plastic rings.

"Hello, girls," said Mrs. Newton. "Goodness, it's the whole club. What's going on?"

"This," replied Kristy, and she handed Jamie's mother one of our fliers.

Mrs. Newton read it carefully. "What a wonderful idea!" she said when she was finished. "You certainly are ambitious, girls."

"We thought it would be fun," said Kristy.

"And a good experience for the children," added Dawn, trying to sound adult.

"I couldn't agree with you more," replied Mrs. Newton. "Jamie starts nursery school in September. This will be perfect for him. He's not around kids his own age much, and I'm afraid school will be sort of a shock for him. If he can at least get used to sharing before he goes to school, that'll be a step in the right direction."

"Great!" I said. "So we can count on Jamie? I mean, he doesn't have to come every time. You don't even have to let us know whether you'll bring him or not. But you're interested?"

"Definitely. He'll be there."

The other club members and I managed to wait until we were safely out of sight of the Newtons' house before we let out little shrieks of excitement.

"Let's go to the Pikes' next," suggested Mary Anne. "Then we can go to the Prezziosos' and the Barretts'. They're all in that neighborhood."

We quickened our pace.

"I bet the Pikes will want to send Claire and Margo," said Stacey as we walked along, "and maybe Vanessa and Nicky. Mallory and the triplets are probably too old." (There are eight Pike kids.)

"I'm sure Mrs. Barrett will want to send Buddy and Suzi," said Dawn thoughtfully, "but I don't know about Marnie. I'd love to have her, but she's not even two years old. That's kind of little."

What nobody was saying (or at least what no one except Mary Anne was saying) was that we hoped Mrs. Prezzioso wouldn't want to send four-year-old Jenny, either. Mary Anne's the only one who likes her. If you ask me, Jenny is a big fat brat. With a capital B.

Kristy rang the Pikes' doorbell, and Mallory answered it. Mallory, the oldest Pike, just had a birthday, and is eleven. She's very good with her younger brothers and sisters. I bet she'll be a baby-sitter herself one day.

"Hi, Mal," said Kristy. "Is your mom here?"

"Yeah, she's out back. Hold on a sec." Mallory yelled for her mother, then let us into the living room. "What's up?" she asked. "How come you're all here? . . . Did one of the triplets do something?"

I giggled. "No. Why?"

"Oh, I don't know. Usually, one of the triplets *has* done something. And when you open the door and see a whole posse of baby-sitters, you think. . . ." Mallory shrugged.

"You think trouble?" asked Kristy.

"Yup."

My friends and I talked to Mrs. Pike and left

one of our fliers with her. Mallory seemed interested in the play group, but before we had left, she walked off glumly.

We looked questioningly at Mrs. Pike. "Is Mallory okay?" asked Mary Anne.

Mrs. Pike nodded. "She's at a funny age, though. She thinks she's too old for some things and too young for most others. I'm sure she'd like to come to the play group, but feels she's too grown up for it."

"Maybe," said Kristy, "she could come for free and be our helper. I don't think we can afford to pay her. But if she wanted to be a sort of baby-sitter-in-training, we'd love to have her. She's always a help."

"That's a lovely idea!" said Mrs. Pike. "I'll talk to her about it. I know she'll be delighted. And," she added as the members of the club were leaving, "I'll probably be sending Claire, Margo, and maybe Nicky to the play group every now and then."

"Great!" we said. "Thanks, Mrs. Pike."

The next stop was the Barretts', but they weren't home, so we left a flier in their mailbox. The three Barretts are Buddy (eight, and a good friend of Nicky Pike), Suzi (four), and Marnie (one, but closer to two). Their parents are separated and Mr. Barrett has moved out, so the kids are having a rough time. Sometimes they can be a handful, but basically they're nice.

We went on to the Prezziosos'. I'm sure Kristy, Stacey, and Dawn were praying that no one would be home there, either. I know I was. But when Mary Anne rang the bell, Mrs. Prezzioso answered it.

She was all dressed up, which wasn't unusual. She likes for her family to look as if they're getting ready to pose for a fashion magazine.

"Hello, girls. What may I do for you?" asked Mrs. P. primly. And then, before one of us could answer, she dropped her voice and whispered, "Our little angel is asleep, so we must keep our voices down." (The little angel is Jenny.)

Mary Anne stepped forward. We had asked her to do all the talking at Jenny's house. "We wanted to let you know," she whispered, "that we're starting a play group."

"A what?" Mrs. P. leaned over, cupping a hand around one ear.

"A play group. And we think it would be perfect for Jenny."

"You think what?"

"We think it would be perfect for Jenny. Here, take a flier."

"A what?"

"A flier." Mary Anne handed her one.

Mrs. P. skimmed it. "I suppose the art projects would be a bit messy, wouldn't they?" Mrs. P. was holding the flier by one corner as if it were a wet painting that was going to leap onto her white suit and smudge it up.

"Well, some might be," I admitted, since I was in charge of art projects. "But . . . um — "

"But we provide smocks," Kristy broke in.

"That's right — smocks," I repeated.

"It sounds nice. I'll have to think about it," Mrs. P. said.

We couldn't wait to get out of there.

"Okay, call us if you have questions," said Kristy.

We went to a few more houses, and then we gathered in my room.

"You know," said Kristy, "I hadn't thought about things like smocks. I wonder if we're forgetting anything else."

"Let's see," said Mary Anne, flipping through the notes she'd been making. "Two picnic tables will be set up in Stacey's yard. We'll each bring our own Kid-Kit with us, so we'll have books and games and puzzles and stuff. Claudia, what kinds of art supplies do you have? Maybe we should buy some things."

"It might be a good idea," I said. "I don't want to use up *all* my materials. And I don't have any construction paper or crayons right now. Just newsprint and pastels."

"Well," Stacey spoke up, "there's money in the treasury, and I guess that's what it's for."

"Right," agreed Kristy. "So if we buy some art supplies, Mary Anne, what shape are we in?"

"I think we're all set," she said.

And I couldn't help adding, "Ready to roll!"

Our play group would begin in just a few days.

CHAPTER 4

On Sunday evening, the night before the first session of the Baby-sitters Club's play group, my parents went out to dinner. They left Mimi and Janine and me on our own, which we don't mind at all. Mimi usually fixes a special meal — not a Japanese meal, but one that we like and don't get to eat very often.

As soon as Mom and Dad had left, Mimi and I went into the kitchen.

"What shall I fix tonight, my Claudia?" Mimi asked.

"Mmm," I said thoughtfully. "We could have spaghetti and meatballs, or we could have breakfast-at-dinner, or — "

"Or I could prepare tiny pizzas."

I laughed. "Mini-pizzas, Mimi," I said. "They're called mini-pizzas."

"That I will never be able to say," replied Mimi, "for Minnie is the mouse. It does not make sense."

"Mouse pizzas!" I exclaimed.

It was Mimi's turn to laugh. "I have an idea," she said. "Would you like a special breakfast-at-dinner? I could prepare waffles in the waffle iron."

(Mimi pronounces *iron* the way it's spelled: eye-ron.)

"Oh, yum! We haven't done that in months! Do we have toppings?" I asked.

"We have butter and syrup and whipped cream and fresh strawberries."

"Oh, boy!"

"Would you please ask your sister if she wants waffles, my Claudia?"

"Okay," I replied. I knew Janine would want waffles. She always goes along with whatever the rest of us have decided.

I found Janine in her room. She was in front of her computer, naturally. A future physicist has to work hard.

"Do you want waffles for dinner?" I asked her abruptly. "That's what Mimi and I chose."

Janine looked up from the keyboard. "You already chose waffles?" she repeated. (I'd just said so, hadn't I?) "Sure. Waffles are fine. How come you didn't ask me what I wanted?"

"I'm asking you now."

"They're fine," Janine said again. Sighing, she turned back to the computer.

I stuck my tongue out at her and ran downstairs.

"Waffles are fine!" I told Mimi.

"Very good. Would you set the kitchen table, please? I will start making the batter."

We went to work. I love to help Mimi in the kitchen. I don't know why Janine doesn't. Of course, we hardly ever remember to ask her.

Soon the table was set. I poured glasses of orange juice and spooned out little bowls of leftover fruit salad. Then I called Janine to the table.

Mimi had put the waffle eye-ron by her plate. She would make the waffles right at the table. The eye-ron was big and old-fashioned. I loved to watch Mimi work it. She would turn it on, then test it with water to see if it was hot enough. If the drops of water bounced off the skillet, it was ready. Then Mimi would brush it with butter, pour on some batter, and close the lid. *Hissss!* Somehow she always knew just when to lift the lid for a perfect golden-brown waffle.

Mimi started cooking and we started eating. When we'd each eaten one waffle, Mimi began again.

"Boy," I said, as the eye-ron hissed, "do I ever have a big day tomorrow."

Janine looked up with interest. "What are you going to do?"

"First of all," I said, "our play group starts in the morning."

"I trust you are prepared for it, both financially and phy— "

"We're all set," I said, cutting Janine off.

"Tell us again how your play group will work, my Claudia," said Mimi.

"Well," I said, "it's kind of like a nursery school, and kind of like a day camp. It will run from nine till twelve-thirty on Monday, Wednesday, and Friday mornings. Anyone who wants to bring their kids by for the morning is welcome to. We won't have an attendance list or anything. We just plan to keep things . . . um. . . ."

"Flexible?" suggested Janine.

"Loose," I said, frowning at her.

"Oh."

"Anyway," I went on, "we've told the Newtons, the Pikes, the Barretts, and all our regular customers about the play group. And we'll have arts and crafts and storytime and stuff. I think everyone will have fun."

"And Janine, what do you plan to do tomorrow?" asked Mimi.

Janine took a large bite of waffle. "The usual," she replied. "School."

"You are enjoying your computer studies?"

"Oh, immensely," said Janine. "Programming is so logical. And once you master the basics, it can be . . . um. . . ."

"Boring?" I suggested.

"Thrilling." Janine gave me a dirty look.

"What are you doing tomorrow, Mimi?" I asked.

"I am not certain, my Claudia. I was invited to a tea, but I have been a little tired. I will see how I feel tomorrow."

"Mimi, you should rest more," I said.

"Yes, you should," added Janine. "You work awfully hard. And you *look* tired."

"Do not worry about me," said Mimi. "Who would like another waffle?"

"Me!" I replied.

"*I,*" said Janine.

"Well, it's not like she didn't know what I meant," I said. "Me, I, what's the difference?"

"The difference is that in the case of an indirect — "

"Girls, that is enough for now," said Mimi gently. "What would you like to do after our breakfast-at-dinner?"

"Watch TV," I said.

"Well, I was going to do some more work," said Janine, "but maybe — I mean, if you both want to, we could play The Trivia Game."

"You are willing to play with us?" Mimi asked Janine, looking as surprised as I felt.

"Yes," she said. "If you *want* to," she repeated hesitantly.

"I would like to play," said Mimi. "How about you, my Claudia?"

I absolutely hate The Trivia Game. I'm no good at it, and Janine knows it, which may be why she asked us to play. I'm not a good student, and I don't care about history or geography or science. What I like are mysteries and art. There are questions in The Trivia Game about art and literature — about paintings and books and stuff — but they're really difficult. I bet hardly any of them are about Nancy Drew.

However, I knew Mimi would want me to play, so I agreed to.

We cleaned up the mess from our breakfast-at-dinner and set up the game on the kitchen table. Janine chose a blue playing piece, Mimi chose yellow, and I chose red. We rolled the dice. I got to go first.

I managed to land on a space for a literature question.

Claudia pulled a card from the box. "The McWhirter twins originated the idea for what book?" she asked. "Hey, you know this one, Claudia! It's easy."

"It is not. And I do not. Know it, I mean."

"Yes, you do. You have this book in your room. You really like it."

Well, now I was feeling stupid. See why I hate this game?

"The Phantom of Pine Hill," I said sarcastically.

"No!" cried Janine. "Be serious. Come on!"

"Janine, tell Claudia the answer, please," said Mimi. "She does not know it."

"It's *The Guinness Book of World Records*, silly."

"It's *The Guinness Book of World Records*, silly," I mimicked her.

Janine ignored me. "My turn!" She rolled the dice and landed on a geography space.

Mimi read her a question. "The equator passes through what three South American countries?"

"Ecuador, Brazil, and Colombia," replied Janine without even thinking. And also managing to say them with a perfect Spanish accent.

What did she do — memorize all five thousand game questions?

Janine rolled again. And again and again and again. She answered one question after another and was halfway to winning before it was Mimi's turn.

Mimi got three right in a row.

My turn again. Unfortunately, I landed on a history spot. That's my worst subject of all.

"Who was known as The Little Corporal?" asked Janine.

I hadn't the vaguest idea. "Kermit the Frog," I replied.

Janine made a face at me. "No. Napoleon Bonaparte." She didn't even check the answer on the back of the card.

"You're making that up!" I accused her. "Show me the card!"

Janine showed me. "See? It *was* Napoleon Bonaparte."

(Who was Napoleon Bone-apart?)

Janine's turn. She went around and around the board, and then managed to land in the special space for her final question.

"Goody. We get to choose the category," I said to Mimi. "Let's give her sports."

"All right," said Mimi, smiling.

I pulled out the next card. "What was Babe Ruth's actual name?"

"Oh, easy," said Janine. "It was George Herman. That's it. I won!"

"Cheater!" I cried. "You looked! You must have looked!"

"I did not," Janine retorted. "I just knew it."

"Nerd!"

Janine slammed the board shut and walked off in a huff.

"Claudia," said Mimi, "that was not nice. It was not called for."

"But Mimi!" I couldn't think of anything to say. Mimi was right. Janine hadn't cheated and I knew it. Janine would never cheat. "Mimi. . . . Oh, you just take Janine's side because she's smarter than I am. Mom and Dad love her more because she's smarter, and I bet you do, too!"

Mimi closed her eyes. "I am very tired, Claudia. I think I will go to bed now."

"But it's only eight o'clock," I said.

"Good-night, Claudia."

Mimi rose and walked slowly toward her bedroom. She closed her door.

CHAPTER 5

I felt terrible. I sat at the kitchen table and stared at the folded-up game board and the scattered playing pieces. Mimi was hardly ever cross with me.

After a while, Janine came back. "Where's Mimi?" she asked.

"She went to bed already."

"Oh. Well, I wanted to say that in case you're wondering, I won't tell Mom and Dad about *The Phantom of Pine Hill.*"

"Huh?"

"You made a mistake earlier."

"While we were playing the game? Yeah, you're right. I made lots of them."

"What I mean is that when I asked you about the book the McWhirter twins originated, and said that you have a copy of it in your room, you answered the question with, *'The Phantom of Pine Hill.'* Now, you know that Mom and Dad don't permit you the Nancy

Drew serial, so you are probably regretting the fact that you accidentally admitted that a book from that serial is in your room. I just wanted to assure you that I will not report this to Mom and Dad. I'm also assuming that Mimi knows about Nancy Drew and has agreed to a pact of silence. Is that correct?"

I wasn't entirely sure what Janine was saying. I had a lot of food hidden in my room, but no cereal. And until Janine brought it up, I hadn't even realized what I'd said about Nancy Drew. However, I decided that "thanks" might be a safe answer.

"Thanks," I said.

"You're welcome. Am I right about Mimi? She knows about Nancy Drew?"

I sighed. "You're right. But you're wrong about the cereal."

Janine looked confused. Then she sat down across from me and shook her head. "Goodness," she said.

"What?"

"I — sometimes I wish I were as close to Mimi as you are."

"Well, maybe if you'd leave your computer alone for fifteen minutes, you'd be closer to all of us. You act like you're married to that thing. Does it make a nice husband?"

Janine rolled her eyes. "That's ridiculous!"

"Oh, so now I'm stupid *and* ridiculous!" I shouted.

Janine opened her mouth, but before she could say anything, we heard a heavy thud. It sounded as if it had come from the first floor, not too far away. Over at Kristy's, that thud could have been her collie, Louie, letting himself inside, or one of her brothers fooling around. But we don't have any pets, and the only other person at home was Mimi.

My eyes met Janine's.

Without a word, as if we were acting as one person, we leaped up from the table and dashed out of the kitchen and through the dining room and living room to Mimi's closed door.

Janine knocked on it.

Right up until that moment, I didn't think anything was *really* wrong. I was sure we would hear Mimi answer, "Come in," maybe sounding a little cross.

But there was no answer.

"Maybe she's asleep already," I suggested.

"Maybe." Janine opened the door a crack, just wide enough for us to see that Mimi's light was on.

"Mimi?" Janine said.

Still no answer.

Janine opened the door all the way.

I screamed.

Janine gasped.

Mimi was lying on the floor in a heap. Before she fell, she must have been getting undressed to go to bed, because she was wearing only her blouse, her slip, and her stockings. Her shoes were lined up neatly next to the closet door.

"She's been murdered!" I shrieked.

"No she hasn't," said Janine. "But I think she had a heart attack or something."

"Is she dead?" I asked.

We both knelt next to Mimi. She looked so little, all crumpled on the floor. Her eyes were shut, and she was as white as a sheet.

Janine took her wrist in one hand. "I can feel her pulse! Claudia, call nine-one-one."

There was a phone on Mimi's nightstand. I lunged for it and called the paramedics. "My grandmother had a heart attack!" I blurted out as soon as someone picked up the phone.

"Tell them she's unconscious," said Janine.

"She's unconscious," I said. "Please hurry." I gave the person our name, address, and phone number, and hung up.

"What should we do?" I wailed.

Janine bit her lip. She was still holding Mimi's hand, patting it gently. "I don't think we're supposed to move her," she said, "but we should keep her warm. Let's cover her with her bathrobe and try to put her slippers on. Then I'll stay in here, and you go wait outside so you can show the paramedics where to come."

"Okay," I replied. I got Mimi's robe and fuzzy slippers out of her closet. Janine put the slippers on while I covered Mimi. Then I ran outside and stood impatiently on our front stoop.

I heard the siren long before I saw the ambulance. At last the ambulance screeched into our driveway, and the attendants hopped out and wheeled a stretcher up the walk in what seemed like two seconds.

"Hurry!" I said. "She's inside. I'll show you where."

I banged through the front door with the attendants at my heels.

"Thank goodness," said Janine when she saw us, but she stayed where she was, sitting with Mimi, until the attendants lifted Mimi onto the stretcher.

"What happened?" one asked me.

"I'm not sure," I replied. "She said she was tired and wanted to go to bed early. So she came in here, and a little while later we heard a thump. My sister and I ran in and found her lying on the floor. We didn't move her," I added, "and we tried to keep her warm."

"You did just fine," said the man.

"What do you think is wrong?" Janine asked him. She glanced worriedly at Mimi's small, still form on the stretcher as the attendants checked her vital signs. "I guessed a heart attack, but perhaps she fell. Or it's possible that she has a head injury."

"I don't think so. There's no sign of trauma to the head," the attendant said. "But don't worry. She's breathing fine, which is a good sign. We'll find out soon enough what's wrong."

While we'd been talking, the paramedics had been wheeling the stretcher toward the front door, and we'd been trailing along behind. They whisked Mimi outside and down the front walk.

"One of you want to come with us?" asked the attendant. "By the way, where are your parents?"

"They've gone out for the evening," Janine replied. "They should be home soon. Claudia, perhaps I should ride with Mimi and you should remain behind to wait for Mom and Dad. You could also try phoning them at *Chez Maurice.*" She turned to the attendant. "When they reach the hospital, should they go to the emergency room?"

"Yes," he replied. "If she's not there any longer, the receptionist will know where she's been taken."

"All right, Claudia?" Janine asked me. "Try the emergency room first." She acted like I was three years old or deaf or something.

"Okay, okay."

The next thing I knew, the ambulance was gone. I felt like sitting down right on the front walk and crying. Instead, I went inside, looked up the number for the *Chez Maurice* restaurant, and dialed it. I must have dialed too fast, though, because the voice that answered said, "Hello, the Arnolds' residence." I hung up and tried again. This time, a perky voice said, *"Bon soir, Chez Maurice."*

"H-hello?" I said. "My name is Claudia Kishi and my parents are having dinner there — I mean, at your restaurant. There's an emergency and I have to talk to them."

"I am *très* sorry, but zey have just left."

"Are you sure?" I asked. "The Kishis? I mean, the Kishi party?"

"Certainement."

I hoped that was French for *certainly.*

"Okay. Thanks," I said.

"Bon nuit."

I walked all around our house, thinking. I decided that it would take Mom and Dad only about fifteen minutes to get home, unless they decided to go somewhere else first. I wandered into Mimi's room, and hung up her skirt and put her shoes in the closet. It occurred to me that she would probably have to stay in the hospital at least overnight, so I found her smallest suitcase and opened it on her bed.

Suddenly I had something to do. I moved quickly, tossing in her nightgown, toothbrush, toothpaste, a Japanese book she was reading, her glasses, and a few other things. To remind her of home, I added the special haiku poem written in Japanese that hangs over her bed.

Then I locked the house and sat down on the front stoop with Mimi's suitcase in my lap. I looked across the street. Both Kristy and Mary Anne's houses were dark. I knew that if they'd been home, they would have come over as soon as the ambulance had driven up.

I waited and waited. All I could think about was my argument with Mimi. I had been mean to her and then she'd had a heart attack. I wondered if you really could give a person a heart attack.

At last I spotted my parents' car down the street. I raced to the end of our driveway and waved frantically to them. When Dad slowed down, I flew into the car, explaining what had happened. Mom grew silent. She didn't say a word as Dad careened through the streets of Stoneybrook.

We reached the hospital in record time. The nurse in the emergency room directed us to the intensive care unit. We took the slowest elevator in the entire world to the fourth floor. When we stepped out, we found Janine in the hall. She was pacing back and forth, wringing her hands, and she'd been crying.

"They won't tell me a thing!" she exclaimed as my parents rushed up to her.

Dad found a nurse and talked quietly with her. Then the four of us sat in a lounge at the end of the hall. My mother couldn't speak. Every time she started to say something, tears filled her eyes and she choked up. Dad held her hand and kept trying to tell her that everything would be okay.

"I've never seen Mom so upset," I whispered nervously to Janine.

"Well, Mimi's her mother," she replied. "We'd be pretty upset if Mom had to be rushed to the hospital."

I nodded. At times like this, Janine didn't seem so bad after all.

A little while later, a doctor came to the

lounge. "It was a stroke," he told us. "A serious one. She's in critical but stable condition. At the moment, she's not able to move or speak, but I've seen people make remarkable recoveries following strokes. We won't know much more for the next twenty-four to forty-eight hours. She's not awake now, and there's nothing you can do for her, so I suggest that you go home, try to get some rest, and come back in the morning."

With heavy hearts, we turned around and went home.

CHAPTER 6

Monday

Today was a good news-bad news day for us baby-sitters. The good news was that ten children came to the first session of our play group and it went really well. The only real problem was Jenny Prezzioso. I should have known. She's a pain. Buddy Barrett, Nicky Pike, and David Michael are kind of wild when they get together, but they're manageable. We're going to have to do something about Jenny, though. Got any ideas, Mary Anne?

The bad news was about Claudia's grandmother, Mimi. It turns out that she had a stroke last night and is in the hospital. The news kind of upset us, but we were able to put our worries aside and run the play group okay, which I guess proves that we're professionals.

W ell, as Dawn said, the play group got off to a great start. The baby-sitters gathered at Stacey's house at eight-thirty. I felt really guilty going, since Mom and Dad were leaving for the hospital to be with Mimi, but Mom had called the intensive care unit to find out how she was doing and the nurse said she was still unconscious. So my parents didn't see any reason for Janine or me to go with them.

Because of all the upset at my house, I was the last one to arrive at Stacey's. I decided I should tell the club members the bad news right off. There was no point in holding it back, and they had a right to know.

When I walked into Stacey's backyard, a boxful of art supplies under one arm, I found everybody busy. Stacey, wearing a pair of knee-length lime-green shorts, matching green high-topped sneakers, and a large white T-shirt with a gigantic taxicab on the front, was setting up benches at the two picnic tables. Mary Anne and Kristy, much more casual dressers, were each wearing blue jean shorts, running shoes, and T-shirts. Mary Anne's shirt, though, was pretty, with a scoop neck and lace edging on the sleeves, while Kristy was wearing an old gray thing that had probably once belonged to Sam or Charlie. It said BOHREN'S MOVERS in faded black letters across the back. Dawn, in a surprisingly New York kind of outfit (she usually goes for California casual), was wearing striped pants with suspenders over a red shirt. The three of them were going through the contents of their Kid-Kits, pulling out storybooks and board games.

"Hi, you guys," I said.

Mary Anne, the most sensitive of all of us, must have been able to tell I was upset just by looking at me, because she immediately said, "What's wrong, Claud? Are you all right?"

"Can you guys come here for a sec?" I replied. "I have to tell you something."

My friends all know Mimi well, since the meetings of the Baby-sitters Club are held at my house. Kristy and Mary Anne know her really well, just because the three of us have grown up together, but Mary Anne is especially close to her because her own mother died years ago. The news was going to upset them all.

Everyone dropped what they were doing and ran to me.

"What is it?" asked Stacey.

"I have bad news," I said, "and I thought you should know right away. Mimi had a stroke last night."

Mary Anne gasped, and Dawn gripped her hand.

"She's okay," I said quickly. "I mean, she can't move, but she's breathing, and the doctor said it's possible she can make a good recovery. We just have to wait and see."

Everyone except Mary Anne relaxed a little. "Can we visit her in the hospital?" she asked, her voice quavering.

I shook my head. "Not yet, anyway. She's in intensive care. Maybe when she's moved to her own room in a different wing."

Mary Anne's lower lip began to tremble.

"Hey!" I said. "I just had an idea. The kids could make get-well cards for Mimi today. Most of them have at least met her."

"That's a great idea!" Kristy chimed in. "We'll combine an art project with . . . with. . . ."

"With learning to care about others," said Dawn. "Perfect. The parents will love it. And more important, Mimi will love the cards."

We felt cheered, and rushed around getting the last things in order. Just before nine o'clock, Kristy gathered us together and said, "I thought we should have a schedule for the day — a loose one. Since it's the first day, we'll just sort of see how things go. Anyway, if this is okay with you guys, I thought we'd start off with an hour and a half when the kids can do whatever they want. Then we'll have music for about twenty minutes, then our snack" — we'd bought canned juice and Saltines — "then stories — maybe one for the older kids and another for the younger ones — and then a group thing, like a game of hide-and-seek or something. If there's any time left before twelve-thirty, they can just play on their own again."

That was Kristy, always in charge. We agreed that her plan sounded good.

"And," continued Kristy, "I think I know who our first kid is going to be."

"Who?" we asked.

"David Michael."

"David Michael!" I exclaimed. "That's great, but why is he coming over? He's got your brothers and your mom, and besides I thought he'd had enough of kids after the week with your cousins over at your house."

"He had," said Kristy, "but Sam and Charlie have summer jobs, and Mom's trying to get the house packed up. Besides, there may be some boys his age here. Nicky Pike or someone."

"Well, fine," I said. And at that moment, David Michael walked uncertainly into the McGills' backyard, clutching three dollars in one fist.

Shortly after David Michael arrived, Charlotte Johanssen came over. Then Mrs. Newton walked Jamie over.

And *then* Mallory Pike showed up with her brother Nicky and her three sisters, Claire, Margo, and Vanessa, plus Suzi and Buddy Barrett and Jenny Prezzioso.

"Mom told me I could help you," Mallory said proudly. "So I started by walking the kids over. I told them about crossing streets and stuff."

"That's wonderful," said Kristy.

"What should I do now?" asked Mallory.

Kristy explained the schedule to her. "Why don't you just kind of keep an eye on the kids while they're playing? You know, stop any fights, or suggest things to them if they seem bored."

"Okay."

Now before I tell you about the trouble that Jenny caused, I should mention how the kids were dressed that morning. Most of them were dressed kind of like Kristy and Mary Anne — in T-shirts and shorts or blue jeans. Suzi Barrett was wearing a faded sunsuit and Claire was wearing short overalls over a striped shirt. Every last one of them was wearing sneakers.

Except for Jenny Prezzioso.

Jenny was wearing a pale pink, spotlessly

clean party dress with puffed sleeves and white smocking across the front. On her feet were lacy white socks and pink Mary Janes.

The very first thing that happened that morning was that Jenny skidded in her Mary Janes and fell on her knees. I have to admit that for just a second I was more worried about the grass stain on the hem of her dress than I was about her knees.

"*Wahh!*" wailed Jenny, not even crying real tears.

"Why don't you take your shoes and socks off?" I suggested. "It's a nice warm day. You won't slip so much in bare feet."

"No," said Jenny stubbornly. "I want to look pretty."

"But when you fell down you got dirt on your dress. See?" I pointed to the grass stain.

Jenny looked at it, considering. Then she looked at her shoes.

"I don't want *to take off* MY PINK SHOES!" she screeched, her voice growing louder with every word.

"Okay, okay, okay."

But that was just the beginning. Jenny didn't know how to share. She wouldn't cooperate with the other children. She said she wanted to play by herself, but when the other kids left her alone, she complained bitterly.

"Nobody likes me," she wailed. She was sitting at a picnic table making a get-well card. She lowered her head onto her arm, the picture of despair.

A blue crayon rolled across the table, heading for her lap.

I dove for it and caught it before it landed on her dress.

"But Jenny, you said you didn't want to play with them," I pointed out.

"Well, I do now!"

"So go play."

"I can't. I'll get my dress dirty."

I rolled my eyes. Jenny was what Mimi would call "a trial." But apart from Jenny, the kids had fun at the play group that morning. And they made a total of nineteen cards for Mimi.

That afternoon I baby-sat for Jamie Newton and his baby sister, Lucy, while Mrs. Newton ran errands and went to a club meeting. I was glad I had so many things to do. Being busy kept my mind off Mimi.

I loved taking care of Jamie and Lucy. The Newtons had been practically the first clients of the Baby-sitters Club. But Jamie was the only little Newton at the time. Then Lucy was born. All of us club members had wondered how Jamie would react to a new baby in the house. We were sure he'd be jealous. And he was a little bit, but only sometimes.

Now the Newtons were planning a big party for Lucy's christening. The party was coming up soon.

"Look at this stuff. Look at all this stuff," Jamie said to me after his mother had left. He led me into the dining room. "Mommy is getting ready to give a party, a big one. And it's all for *her*." Jamie nodded his head toward the second floor, where Lucy was taking her afternoon nap.

The Newtons did seem to be getting ready for a very large party. The dining room table was covered with boxes of crackers, cans of peanuts, tins of candies, stacks of napkins; plus glasses, silverware, plates, a punch bowl and cups, serving spoons, and more.

"You know what?" I said. "When you were Lucy's age, your parents gave a great big party after your christening."

"They did?" Jamie brightened. Then he frowned. "But I don't remember it!" he said loudly.

"Shh." I put a finger to my lips. "The baby — "

"I know," said Jamie sullenly. "The baby is sleeping."

Uh-oh, I thought. This doesn't look good.

But when Lucy woke up a little later, Jamie was the first to hear her crying. He leaped up from the floor, where we were playing a hot game of Candy Land, and ran to her room. I followed. When I caught up with him, I found him standing by her crib, one arm between the slats, patting her on the back and saying softly, "Claudy's here. Claudy's here. You can stop crying now, Lucy. Claudy's here."

It was a nice scene. I filed it away in my memory.

I got Lucy dressed and gave her some juice, and then I suggested that we take a walk. Jamie wanted to go over to my house. He likes my art supplies, but he also likes Mimi, and I think what he really wanted was to see for himself that she was actually gone. I wasn't sure how much "in the hospital" meant to him.

So I put Lucy in her stroller, and we walked to my house.

"Is Mimi here?" asked Jamie as I was unlocking the front door.

"Nope. Remember — I said she's in the hospital. She's sick."

Jamie mulled that over and went on to a different subject. "Is anybody here?"

"Just us," I told him. "Want to look at my paints?"

Jamie shook his head. "Let's play outside."

I sat on the lawn and played with Lucy while Jamie turned somersaults in the grass. Presently a car pulled up and Janine got out.

" 'Bye!" she called to her carpool. "See you tomorrow!"

Jamie ran over to me as the car drove away. "Who's that?" he whispered.

"That's Janine, my sister. You know her."

Jamie decided she was safe. "Hi-hi," he said to Janine.

"Hello, Jamie," she replied. She looked at Lucy and me. "Hi, Claudia. . . . Oh, look at you, Lucy. You're so big!"

"How was school?" I asked.

Janine sat down and began playing pat-a-cake with Lucy. "It was very exciting," she replied. "Physics and astronomy are a fascinating combination of science — "

"Ja*nine*," I exclaimed, irritated.

"What?" She let go of Lucy's hands.

"I don't believe you!" I exploded.

"*What?*" Janine said again. She stood up.

I stood, too, and we faced each other.

Jamie looked on with interest.

"You didn't even ask about Mimi," I accused her. "Or about Mom."

"You didn't give me a chance. You inquired how school was. Besides, I know how both of them are. I phoned Mom from the campus this afternoon. There's no appreciable difference in Mimi. And Mom's . . . well, she's all right.''

"Why didn't you tell me?"

"I repeat — you did not give me a chance."

"Janine, you are so mean!"

Janine glared at me. Then, to everybody's surprise, I actually raised my hand as if to hit her, but I dropped it quickly. (Jamie was now wide-eyed with fascination. He was looking back and forth between Janine and me.)

Janine shook her head. Then she stomped into the house.

"Mean Janine," I muttered. "Come on, Jamie. Let's go."

Janine had spoiled my whole afternoon.

CHAPTER 7

When I finished at the Newtons', I ran home and just made it in time for the meeting of the Baby-sitters Club. I found Kristy and Mary Anne waiting on the front stoop, their chins in their hands.

"Why aren't you guys inside?" I asked. "You know you can always go to my room if I'm late."

"We didn't think anyone was here," said Kristy gloomily.

"Well, you're almost right," I said. "The only one here is Janine."

"No Mimi," said Mary Anne.

"Nope. No Mimi," I said.

The Monday afternoon meeting of the Baby-sitters Club was sort of glum.

"What are we going to do about Jenny?" I asked when everyone had arrived. I searched my hiding places and found a bag of gumdrops, which I passed around.

"She does cause problems," agreed Mary Anne.

"She starts fights with the other kids," Stacey pointed out. "Sometimes she doesn't even mean to, but she does anyway. By not sharing or something. I saw Claire Pike ask Jenny for a red crayon that she wasn't using. When Jenny wouldn't give it to her, Claire got mad, turned around, and whacked Suzi Barrett."

"If we could at least get her mother to dress her in play clothes, it would be helpful," said Kristy. "One of us should talk to Mrs. Prezzioso."

"Yes, *one* of us should," I said pointedly. We all looked at Mary Anne.

"*Me?*" she squeaked.

"You're the only one who likes her," Kristy said bluntly.

Mary Anne made a face. "But she doesn't *have* any real play clothes. I know that for a fact. Maybe we should just make her wear one of the painting smocks all morning."

The phone began to ring then, and we stopped to set up some appointments. By the time we'd finished, we'd half forgotten about Jenny.

"You know what would usually happen right about now during a meeting?" Mary Anne asked. She went on without waiting for an answer, "Mimi would come in for some reason — to ask us if we needed anything, or to remind us not to eat too much before dinner."

"Yeah," I said. "I think I'll call Mom at work and see if anything's going on." Kristy has this rule about not making personal calls during club meetings, but I knew she'd let me break it. I didn't even bother to ask if it was okay.

I picked up the phone and dialed my mother's office at the library.

"Hello!" called a voice.

"Mom?" I asked.

"Claudia?"

"Mom?"

"Hey, dope, your mom's *home!*" Kristy said, nudging me in the ribs and grinning.

I dropped the phone. "Mom?" I could hear her coming up the stairs.

My mother appeared in the doorway. "Hi, girls," she said. She looked awfully tired.

"How's Mimi?" I asked right away.

"Good news. She just woke up. She can't move or speak yet, but she's awake."

"All *right!*" exclaimed Kristy.

"Can I see her?"

"Yes. Family members may see her one at a time for about ten minutes each. We'll go back to the hospital after supper. Speaking of which, Claudia, I'll need your help with supper tonight. I'm afraid we've all gotten awfully used to having Mimi take care of us." Mom began to sound sort of teary again.

The meeting broke up soon after that, and I joined my mother in the kitchen. "Where's Janine?" I asked. "Can't she help, too?"

"Oh, I didn't even bother to ask her," replied Mom distractedly. "I'm sure she's busy with her schoolwork."

And what did my mother think the Baby-sitters Club was, I wondered. A game? But I didn't say anything. I looked through the freezer. "Here are some frozen French fries. And here are some hamburger patties. We could heat these up."

"Fine," said Mom. "Help me make a salad, honey. Then we'll be ready."

After our makeshift dinner, Mom and Dad and Janine and I drove to the hospital. The closer I got to Mimi, the more worried I became. All I could think about was the mean way I had behaved. I clutched the nineteen get-well cards in my hands and kept hearing my ugly words over and over again, and Mimi's quiet voice telling me good-night. She hadn't called me "my Claudia," so she really must have been hurt. What would I say when I saw her?

"Mom, can Mimi hear us?" I asked.

"Well, that's a silly question," said Janine.

Dad glanced at her in the rearview mirror. "I'd be interested in your answer, Dr. Kishi," he said.

"The answer," said Janine, "is, Of course she can hear us."

"According to the neurologist, the answer is, We think she can hear us, but we're not sure how well."

"Oh," said Janine quietly.

"Why did you want to know, Claudia?" Dad asked.

"I . . . I just wanted to be sure she could hear me when I — when we talk to her."

We drove on in silence.

At the hospital, Mom and Dad led Janine and me to Mimi's room.

Mom went in first, looking as nervous as a cat.

"Can I please go in next?" I begged, when she came out.

"*May* I," Janine corrected me, glancing warily into the room.

I ignored her. I don't think she was even aware that she'd said it.

"Sure," Mom answered me. "Watch the clock on the wall, honey, and stick to the ten-minute time limit. The nurses are strict about that. And don't be frightened. There's a lot of equipment in the room. Just remember that it's there to help Mimi."

I crept into the room. It was dim and quiet except for the hum of machinery. Mimi was hooked up to a couple of things with TV screens on the fronts. There were no pictures on the screens, though. Just lighted dots that kept zigzagging from one side to the other. Next to her bed was a stand with a plastic sack of clear liquid at the top. A tube ran from the sack down into a needle that was stuck into Mimi's wrist. I shuddered.

Mimi looked like a little doll lying in the metal bed with the scary machines around her.

I tiptoed over to her bed. "Mimi?" I whispered.

Mimi's eyes were open, but she wasn't quite looking at me.

"Mimi?" I whispered again.

Nothing. The same dull stare. It was spooky.

Too spooky. I couldn't stand her eyes. So I backed away. I backed all the way out of the room, knocking into the wastebasket as I went.

"Claudia?" said my mother. "Are you all right?"

"You go, Janine," I said, ignoring Mom's question.

I stood by the doorway holding the nineteen get-well cards, and watched Janine. Mom stood right behind me with her hand on my shoulder.

I saw Janine's face as she took in the machines. I saw her eyes widen as she took in Mimi's blank stare. But Janine stayed where she was. She began talking to Mimi just as if they were sitting across from each other over cups of tea. She talked quietly to her for the full ten minutes. I wish I could have heard what she was saying.

When Janine came out, Mom looked at me, wordlessly asking if I wanted to go in again.

I shook my head. Then, tears welling up in my eyes, I fled down the hall to the lounge and sat in front of the soda machines until it was time to go home.

The next evening, we went back. I'd spent all day talking to myself, saying things like, "Don't be selfish" or "Don't be a baby. Mimi needs you."

So the second time I went into her room, once again bringing the get-well cards, I was prepared. I tried to ignore the dim light and the humming machines. And I tried to remember Mimi the way she was before the stroke.

I looked around the room.

In a corner was a wooden armchair with vinyl cushions. I pulled it next to the bed and leaned over. I forced myself to look into Mimi's eyes.

"Hi, Mimi," I said.

She blinked her eyes, but that was all. Had she heard me? How awful not to be able to wave or smile or anything.

"Mimi, I'm only allowed to stay for ten minutes," I told her. "So I'll tell you what's been going on." I paused. "Well, we had our first play group. Do you remember what that was?"

Mimi blinked her eyes, but I noticed that they were focused somewhere on the ceiling.

"Well, you probably do. Anyway, it went fine. And guess what the art project was. The kids made get-well cards for you. They were all really sorry to hear that you're in the hospital. A lot of the kids made two or three cards. I brought them with me. This one is from David Michael. See?" I held it up. "It says, 'Get will soon Mini.' And this is from Margo Pike. She's just learning to write, so the letters spell 'HGDOMYLSP,' but she translated for me, and they mean, 'Please feel better. I hope you can come home soon. Love, Margo.' She drew a picture of a fireman for you. And Buddy Barrett made this one: 'Der Claudi's granmohter plese fell better verry soon and com back becase we want you to plese fell better verry soon. Yours truly, Hamilton Barrett, Junior.' It took him twenty minutes to write that."

I showed Mimi the rest of the cards. Then I said, "I think we'll put them over here on the windowsill. They'll kind of cheer up the room."

I lined the cards up. It was hard to keep thinking of things to tell Mimi. I wasn't used to one-sided conversations. Kristy would have done fine, since she could talk the ear off of a cornstalk, and Janine had done okay the night before, but I'm not a big talker. If I knew for sure that Mimi could hear me it would have been a little easier, but she wasn't giving any signs. The only movement I'd seen was when she blinked her eyes.

Her eyes! I had an idea.

I stood up. "Hey, Mimi," I said, leaning way over and looking right into her eyes. "If you can hear me, blink your eyes."

Mimi blinked.

I gasped. But maybe it was just an accident. She'd been blinking a lot already.

I tried something else. "Mimi, if my name is Claudia, blink *two* times."

Mimi blinked twice.

"You *can* hear!" I exclaimed. "Oh, wow!

69

Now we can talk! Mimi, this will be our code. One blink means yes. Two blinks mean no, okay?"

Mimi blinked once.

"Do you like your get-well cards?" I asked.

One blink.

"Do you know you're in the hospital?"

One blink.

"Mimi, my ten minutes are almost up, but I have to tell you something really, really important. I . . . I'm sorry I yelled at you the other night. I didn't mean what I said. I love you very much, and I'm sorry. Do you understand?"

One blink.

"Oh, I wish I could hug you," I said tearfully, "but I don't see how. Too many machines and tubes. Okay?"

One blink.

Mom was signaling to me from the hallway. I had to leave. I rushed out and told everyone about the blinks. Dad got hold of a doctor, and Mom ran in to "talk" with Mimi. It was exciting.

Still, when we returned home that evening, we were silent and sad. It was awful that Mimi had to talk by blinking her eyes. And the doctors still didn't know how much better she would get.

I wandered around my room for a while, and then decided I wanted some company. Mom and Dad were on the phone with relatives, so I peered into Janine's room. She was at her computer. The keys were clackety-clacking away a mile a minute. The funny thing was, she looked like she was crying a little, but when I called to her, she didn't answer. I guess she couldn't hear me over the noise.

CHAPTER 8

Wednesday

Well, Karen Brewer strikes again. Leave it to Karen. When she's around, things are never dull. Today was the second session of our play group and Andrew and Karen came to it. Watson's ex-wife needed a last-minute sitter for them, so she called Watson and he decided to drop them off at Stacey's.

In the past, Karen has scared other kids with stories about witches, ghosts, and martians. Today, she had a new one — a monster tale. But it was a monster tale with a twist, as you guys know. I'm not sure there's anything we can do about Karen. The thing is, she usually doesn't mean to scare people. She just has a wild imagination.

But, oh boy, when Karen and Jenny got together....

I'm sure glad Kristy likes Karen Brewer so much, since they're stepsisters now. And I like Karen myself, but she's a handful! She's not the unpleasant kind of handful that Jenny is, but she's still a lot to manage.

Anyway, as Kristy said, Karen and Andrew needed last-minute looking-after, so Watson dropped them off at Stacey's. They were a little late, and were the last ones to arrive at the play group.

We had almost the same group of kids as we'd had on Monday. Mallory came over with Claire, Margo, and Nicky (but not Vanessa); Jenny; and Buddy Barrett (but not Suzi). David Michael, Charlotte, and Jamie all showed up. And so did Nina and Eleanor Marshall, two little girls the club sits for sometimes. Nina is four and Eleanor's two. Eleanor was the baby of the group, but she seemed to have fun.

When Karen and Andrew arrived, the kids (except for Jenny) were playing happily. Charlotte, Claire, and Margo were making collages by gluing foil stars and colored tissue paper onto pieces of cardboard. Nina was looking at a book with Eleanor. Buddy, Nicky, and David Michael were roaring around, playing something Nicky had invented called Blast into

Superspace. And Jamie was building with his Legos, which he'd brought over.

Mallory was helping out at the art table, but what were the five of us baby-sitters doing? We were gathered around Jenny, trying to convince her to put on a smock. The smock was a shirt that had belonged to Stacey's father. It was old but clean, and in perfectly good condition. Jenny refused to wear it.

The day before, Mary Anne had somehow found the courage to phone Mrs. Prezzioso and suggest that she dress Jenny in play clothes. And today Jenny had shown up in Mrs. P.'s idea of play clothes, a brand new white sundress with ruffles around the bottom, trimmed with pale pink ribbon and white lace, and brand new white sandals. The sandals were the fancy kind, more like shoes with holes punched on top in a pretty design.

We baby-sitters were horrified.

"All in white!" Stacey had moaned. She clapped a hand to her forehead.

"And the dress is freshly ironed," added Dawn, awestruck.

"These are play clothes?" cried Kristy. "Look at the other kids: shorts, shorts, shorts, blue jeans, shorts, shorts, overalls" — that was Eleanor — "shorts, jeans, very old sundress" — that was Margo. "And all of us and Mallory are in, well, *fairly* old clothes." (Some of us looked nicer than others.)

"Come on, Jenny," I said. "Just put the smock on."

"No."

"Why not?"

"This is my new dress. I want everyone to see it."

"We've all seen it. It's beautiful," I told her. "And if you put the smock on, you can keep your dress beautiful — all nice and clean like it is now." I held the smock out to her.

"No."

"Look, this can be *your* smock," Stacey suggested. "Your special smock. Nobody else will have one like it. Claudia could even put your name on it."

This is what was going on when Karen and Andrew showed up.

Karen marched jauntily into the yard, with Andrew several steps behind her.

I was relieved to see that both were wearing shorts. And sneakers.

"Here we are!" Karen announced gaily. (Watson had phoned Kristy earlier to say that they'd be coming.)

"Hiya, Karen. Hi, Andrew," said Kristy. She

turned away from Jenny to give them each a hug. When Kristy stood up, Karen peered around her and spotted Jenny.

"Who's that?" she asked, frowning.

"That's Jenny Prezzioso," Kristy told her.

"How come she's all dressed up? Is she going to a birthday party?"

"This is my new dress," Jenny said proudly. She whirled around, making the ruffles fan out. "Isn't it pretty?"

"I don't know," replied Karen. She narrowed her eyes. "You'll have to keep it awfully clean."

"So what?" said Jenny.

"So what?" Karen mimicked her.

It was time to step in. "Karen," I said, "David Michael's over there." I pointed him out. "Why don't you go play with him and his friends?"

Karen glanced at Jenny again. It was instant hatred, I could tell. I've seen it happen before. It was like that with me and Beverly Mc-Maniman in fourth grade. We were enemies the entire year.

"Okay," said Karen. She started to walk away. But as she left she called over her shoulder — *very* casually — to Jenny, "Watch out for the monster." Then she kept on walking.

"What monster?" Jenny cried.

"Karen," Kristy said warningly.

Karen kept on walking, as if she hadn't heard them.

"What monster?" Jenny shrieked. She ran after Karen.

"Hey, come back!" I called. "Your smock!"

Now Jenny was pretending not to hear.

Since Karen was older than Jenny and had longer legs, she reached David Michael quickly.

I looked at the other club members as Jenny hurried to catch up with Karen. "Now what?" I said.

"Oh, let them go," replied Dawn.

"But Jenny's dress — "

"Maybe we should just let it get dirty," said Mary Anne unexpectedly.

We looked at her in surprise. That was a very un-Mary-Anne-like thing to say.

"Well, what does Mrs. P. think goes on at a play group?" she asked.

"Yeah," I said. "And what does Jenny *do* all day when she's at home? Doesn't she ever get dirty?"

"We have our reputations to think about," said our president nervously. "If Jenny goes home with a ruined dress, Mrs. P. might be really upset. She might tell Mrs. Pike and Mrs. Pike might — "

"Eeee!"

"What was that?" I asked.

Before we could find out who had shrieked — and why — David Michael ran up to us and said breathlessly, "What's big and red and eats rocks? A big, red rock-eater, that's what!"

We looked at the group in the corner of the yard. They seemed fine. David Michael had run back to them, and the three boys and Karen were talking earnestly, probably telling jokes (although we couldn't be sure). Jenny listened from a few feet away.

"We can't worry about Jenny all day," I pointed out. "We better get to work."

Kristy joined Jamie with his Legos, Mary Anne sat down with Nina and Eleanor, and Dawn and Stacey wandered over to the kids at the art table.

I decided to keep an eye on the entire group. That was when I noticed Andrew. He was still standing at the entrance to Stacey's backyard.

"Hey, Andrew," I said, approaching him.

Andrew looked at his feet and dug the toe of one sneaker into the grass. He's very shy.

"Andrew, does anyone ever call you Andy?" I asked.

"Mommy calls me Andy-Pandy," he said.

"Would it be all right if I called you Andy?"

He nodded.

"Good," I said. "Let's go see what your sister's doing." I took Andrew by the hand and led him toward the group of kids. I thought that all of them looked kind of frightened.

"What's going on, you guys?" I asked brightly.

The kids looked up. They saw Andrew and me, and they all began screaming. Then they ran away.

"What on earth?" I exclaimed.

"Monster!" shrieked Jenny.

Andrew and I ran to her.

Jenny let out another shriek. "Get that boy away from me!" she cried, pointing to Andrew. "He's a monster!"

"Oh, Jenny," I said. "A *mon*ster? Where did you get that idea? He's just Andrew."

"No, no! He turns into a monster! She said so." Now Jenny was pointing to Karen.

"Oh, brother," I said. "Karen, come here right this minute."

Karen crept over. She stopped about fifteen feet away from me.

"Come *here*," I repeated.

Karen shook her head. Then, "What time is it?" she asked.

"Almost ten o'clock. Why?"

"Because," replied Karen, trembling, "Morbidda Destiny put a spell on Andrew last weekend. At ten o'clock today he's going to turn into a monster."

Andrew looked up at me and smiled. "Grrrrrr," he said.

"Aughhh!" screamed Karen, Jenny, David Michael, and most of the kids in the yard. They'd all been listening. They didn't know that Morbidda Destiny was a weird old neighbor of Karen's whom Karen thought was a witch. But they believed that Andrew was going to turn into a monster.

Kristy glanced at me and shrugged.

"All right," I said, looking at my watch. "In a few seconds it will be ten o'clock. Let's count down together, and you'll see that Andrew is just Andrew."

"Ten," I said, "nine, eight" — the kids joined in nervously — "seven, six, five, four, three, two . . . *one!*"

"*Aughh!*" The kids had all covered their eyes and were screaming.

"Hey, Kristy. Whistle," I told her.

Kristy put her fingers in her mouth and let loose with an ear-blasting whistle. Everyone stopped screaming. They looked at Andrew.

"*Don't growl,*" I whispered fiercely to him. Andrew obeyed.

Slowly, things returned to normal. Jenny,

however, seemed quite subdued. Later, Andrew saw us sitters fussing with Jenny about her smock again. "Put it on," he told her impatiently.

Jenny's eyes grew wide. She grabbed for the smock.

I grinned. "Andy," I whispered, "tell her to wear it every time she comes to Stacey's."

"Grrr," said Andrew. "You wear that . . . wear that every day."

"Okay," said Jenny. "Okay."

Across the yard, I saw Karen cover her mouth with her hands and giggle.

CHAPTER 9

One evening, when Mom and Dad came home from work, Mom was grinning. She looked like somebody who knew a secret.

"Hi, honey," she said. "Oh, you started supper! Thank you. That's wonderful."

"You've been acting very responsibly lately," Dad added.

Responsibility is sort of a touchy subject with my parents and me. For as long as I can remember, I've heard, "If you'd just do your homework when it's assigned . . ." or, "If you'd be on time for once . . ." or, "If you'd just think ahead the way Janine does. . . ."

And now Dad was telling me I was acting responsibly. Well, it was true that I'd started dinner several times recently, and I'd spent a lot of time with Mimi in the hospital. On the other hand, I'd given Mimi the stroke in the first place. I'd lost my temper and been rude to her. That certainly wasn't very responsible.

"Hey, Mom, how come you're smiling?" I asked. "Something happened, didn't it?"

"I'll say," she replied. "Where's your sister?"

"Guess."

"Working at her computer."

"Well, close. She's upstairs studying, or at least she was earlier. Do you want me to get her?"

"Please. Dad and I will finish getting dinner ready."

I ran upstairs. Janine's door was closed, so I knocked on it.

"Come in!" she called.

"Thanks for helping me with dinner," I greeted her sarcastically.

Janine frowned. "You didn't tell me you were starting dinner. I would have helped if I'd known."

"Well, you have a watch, don't you? It's six o'clock. Couldn't you have guessed?" But I felt bad. It was true. I hadn't asked Janine for help, and I didn't make dinner every night, so why should she have known?

"Have you come into my bedroom merely to torment me?" asked Janine. "Or do you have some other purpose?"

"Some other purpose," I mumbled.

Janine was seated at her desk. Three fat textbooks were open in front of her. A half-filled sheet of lined paper was in her hand. At her feet were several balls of crumpled paper. She glanced at the paper in her hand, as if she couldn't bear to keep her eyes off it for very long.

"Well?" said Janine.

"Mom said she has good news. She wants us to come downstairs right away."

"Very well."

Janine placed bookmarks in her texts and slid the paper into a folder. Then she followed me to the kitchen.

Mom and Dad were just dishing up the supper I'd started, which was frozen carrots (I mean, formerly frozen carrots), a lettuce salad, and baked chicken.

"Claudia says you have some news," Janine said, slipping into her chair.

"Yes, we do," replied Mom. She waited until the four of us were seated. Then she went on. "As you know, at first Mimi couldn't move at all, though she has been able to move her left side a little bit recently. Well, today, using her left hand, she actually fed herself part of her lunch, *and* she tried to speak. Several times."

"Oh, boy!" I cried. "That's great! Isn't it?"

"It was good enough to get her out of

intensive care," said Dad, smiling.

"Where is she now?" asked Janine. She was smiling, too. In fact, we were all smiling. We probably looked sort of goofy.

"She's in a regular room," Dad replied. "A private one."

"Can we visit her tonight?" I asked.

"*May* we?" Janine, Mom, and Dad all corrected me at once.

"*Sheesh*," I said. "*May* we visit her?"

"We certainly may," said Mom.

With that, dinner was eaten in a jiffy. Janine had looked busy before, but we didn't hear a peep from her about having to finish any work. She helped me pick a bouquet of flowers from our back garden for Mimi, and then the four of us were off to the hospital.

Mom and Dad showed Janine and me to a different wing on the same floor as the intensive care unit where Mimi had been. This time, we could all go in to see her at once.

Mimi looked much better. There was no needle stuck in her wrist, and most of the machines were gone. Also, she was sort of sitting up (actually, the folding bed was making her sit up), and someone had washed and fixed her hair.

When we filed into the room, Mimi tried to

smile and got about halfway there. Then she raised her left hand in greeting.

"Hi, Mimi!" I cried. "You can wave! That's great!" I rushed to one side of the bed and kissed her cheek.

Janine stood on the other side of the bed, while Mom and Dad sat in chairs.

"Are you feeling better?" I asked Mimi.

She blinked her eyes once.

"Good," I said.

"Mom said that you are partially able to feed yourself," Janine spoke up.

In answer, Mimi raised her left hand again and wiggled the fingers.

I glanced at Mom and Dad, wondering whether it would be all right to say anything about the fact that Mimi had tried to speak. I wanted to tell her how great that was, but before I could say anything, Mimi made a gurgling sound in her throat.

Janine and I both leaned forward quickly.

"What did you say?" I asked.

More gurglings. Then a sort of "mmm" sound.

I looked helplessly at Mom, who got to her feet and came over to the side of the bed.

"I'm sorry, Mother," said Mom. "We couldn't quite catch that."

"Maybe she could write it down," I suggested.

"I don't know," said Mom. "She's not left-handed."

"I think we ought to attempt it," said Janine. "Perhaps it would work."

"All right," said Mom. She looked at Mimi. "Mother, do you think you could write down what you want to say?"

Mimi frowned slightly, then blinked once.

"Here," said my father, standing up. "I've got a pad and pencil."

"I think she'll need something bigger," I said.

Everyone looked at me. "Why do you think that?" asked Dad curiously.

"I just — just do." I've had enough trouble in school to know what will be easy, and what will be difficult.

"I'll see what I can find," said Dad.

He headed for the nurses' station and returned with a couple of pieces of notebook paper. Janine propped Mimi's arm up on the little table that slid across the bed. She put Dad's pencil in her hand and the paper on the table, holding it in place for Mimi.

Mimi appeared to be concentrating very hard. After several moments she began to write. It took forever. When she finally stopped, this is what was on her paper:

HAdyd S3 To KOQOMO

We all stared at it.

"Mom," I whispered, pulling her away from the bed, "something's wrong. I know Mimi's right-handed, but why is everything all mixed around and upside down?"

Mom shook her head slightly and put a finger on my lips. She turned back to Mimi. Dad and Janine were still puzzling over the message.

"I think the first word is *happy*," Janine was saying.

"If I'm not mistaken," Mom broke in, "she's saying she's happy to see you girls. *Kodomo* is Japanese for *child* or *children*."

"Why didn't she just say *children?* Or use our names?" I asked.

"I don't know, honey," replied Mom.

"Well, what's going on in here?" came a hearty voice.

Standing in the doorway to Mimi's room was one of her doctors.

"Girls, you remember Dr. Marcus, don't you?" asked Mom. "Dr. Marcus, this is Janine, and this is Claudia."

Dr. Marcus stepped into the room and shook hands with Janine and me. Then he went to Mimi's side. "I hear you've been making lots of progress today," he said.

Mimi blinked once and waved her left hand.

The rest of us stood back while Dr. Marcus took a look at Mimi. When he was done, he went into the hall and my parents joined him for a brief conference. They took Mimi's note with them. Janine and I stayed behind, talking to Mimi. I told her I was turning into a cook, but that I wasn't nearly as good as she was.

When we were home that evening, Dad told us what the doctor had said.

"Mimi is making average progress."

"Just average?" I asked in disappointment.

"Average is fine."

Not when it's a C in school, I thought.

"She's going to start having therapy," added Mom.

"What sort of therapy?" Janine wanted to know.

"All sorts," replied Mom. "Physical, speech, and occupational. Occupational will help her relearn basic skills such as eating, dressing, and brushing her teeth. When she's well enough, they'll help her with cooking or sewing or whatever. But they'll start small — with anything that's giving her trouble. Right now her brain is just sort of mixed up. The doctor thinks she'll make plenty of improvement, but it will take time."

"But — but it's like she's a little kid!" I sputtered.

"In a way, that's right," replied Dad. "Only it won't, for instance, take her five or six years to be able to read and write again. Her brain already knows how. It's just having trouble sending the proper messages to the rest of her body."

"The hospital is going to provide her with some therapy every day," said Mom. "But Dr. Marcus said that the more stimulation she gets, the faster she'll improve. Your father and I realized that if we each took a couple of hours off from work every afternoon, one or the other of us would be here from about two o'clock, when she'll return from therapy, until six."

"Well . . ." Janine said slowly.

But I interrupted her. "I'll spend the mornings with her! I can switch to Saturday art classes." It was the least I could do, considering I'd nearly killed her.

"Oh, that would be *wonderful*," said Mom enthusiastically. "Just what she needs."

Janine looked a little disappointed. "Oh," she said, "I suppose it *would* be an exercise in futility to attempt to rearrange my course schedule. But what about your club's play group, Claudia?"

I paused. Good question. Then I put my nose in the air. "What's a silly old play group compared to Mimi?" I said loftily. But for some reason, I didn't feel nearly as good about my decision as I sounded.

CHAPTER 10

Wednesday

Today's play group was over hours ago and I'm still laughing about what went on. Now this is an example of something great that probably could never have happened in New York City. It started when David Michael brought Louie to the play group. Just to set things off on the wrong foot, it turns out that Jenny is afraid (and I mean terrified) of dogs. Remember that for the future, you guys. Then David Michael decided we needed to give Louie a bath. That's when the trouble really began. When the morning was over, Louie was the only one who was both clean and dry. Thank goodness Jenny was wearing her smock.

Claudia — we miss you!

It was nice of Stacey to say that. I missed the play group, too. But Mimi was more important. Luckily, the other club members agreed with me. They'd been disappointed when I'd said I'd have to drop out of the play group. But they'd understood. They all wanted Mimi to get well as much as I did.

Anyway, Stacey called to tell me about the Louie-washing. When she got to certain points in the story, she would start laughing again, and laugh so hard she could barely speak.

The reason Louie went to the McGills' was that Mrs. Thomas made him go. The Thomases were moving the next day, and Louie was in the way. Anyway, Mrs. Thomas sent David Michael to the play group with Louie in tow. And she sent over three dollars for each of them. The money was accompanied by a note that said:

Dear Kristy,
Please, please, PLEASE watch Louie this
morning and don't send him home before
12:30. He nosed through the garbage right
after you left, and strewed spaghetti all over
the kitchen floor. Thank you.
Love, Your Old Mom

When David Michael came over, it was about nine-thirty, and Jenny, Mallory, Claire, Margo and Nicky, Suzi and Buddy, Nina and Eleanor, and Jamie had already arrived. Louie was kind of wound up, so he gallumphed into Stacey's backyard, barking happily.

"Ohhhhhaughhhhh!" shrieked Jenny, as Louie bounded over to the art table and stuck his wet nose in her face.

"Uh-oh," said Stacey. "David Michael, move him away from the art stuff, okay?"

"Okay," said David Michael. "Here," he added, handing Kristy the money and note from their mother. Then he tugged on Louie's collar and hauled him to another part of the yard.

"What's wrong?" Stacey asked Jenny, picking her up.

Jenny was wearing her smock. She had barely taken it off, even at home, since the time Andrew the monster had told her to wear it every day. Apparently, her mother was somewhat upset about that, because with the smock on, she could hardly show off Jenny's gorgeous wardrobe.

"I don't like him," Jenny wailed.

"Louie won't hurt you. He's a nice old dog — a collie. See all his fluffy fur? Isn't he pretty?"

"No," said Jenny, shaking her head and

wrinkling her nose. She buried her face against Stacey.

Stacey had to admit that Louie wasn't looking his best. He needed to be brushed, and he had spaghetti sauce on his nose and feet.

"Well," she said lamely, "he's nice, anyway." She set Jenny back on the bench at the picnic table.

Jenny raised her head and looked around nervously. "Where's that dog now?" she asked.

"Over there. See? Jamie's petting him. Jamie doesn't mind old Louie."

"He's dirty," said Jenny. "He's a messy-face."

"Well, you're protected. You've got your smock on."

"Monster smock," whispered Jenny.

Stacey sighed. She left Jenny with Mallory and wandered over to Jamie and David Michael. Kristy joined them.

"How do you think Louie's going to like his new neighborhood?" Stacey asked Kristy.

"Oh, I think he'll like it all right. It's too bad he's not a purebred Shih Tzu or Pomeranian, though. Or a purebred anything. He'd fit in better with all those rich, snobby dogs. I bet those dogs don't even have doghouses in their backyards. I bet they have little dog mansions."

Stacey laughed. Then she said, "I thought Louie was a purebred collie."

"Nope," replied Kristy. "One of his grand-fathers was a sheep dog."

"How would anyone ever know that?" asked Stacey.

"Rich people find out all sorts of things you wish they didn't know," said Kristy.

"Will they know he got into the spaghetti this morning?" asked David Michael.

"Anyone would know that," Stacey replied. "He looks, smells, and feels like spaghetti sauce."

"Well, then," said David Michael, "do you have a tub?"

"A tub?" asked Stacey. "What for?"

"We'll have to give him a bath."

Stacey looked at Kristy.

Kristy began to smile. "It's not a bad idea," she said.

"And," added David Michael, "we have to fix him up."

"Huh?" said Kristy.

"You know, fluff his fur, put some ribbons on him, find his plaid leash. I don't want any of those rich people or rich dogs making fun of him tomorrow," David Michael said fiercely.

Stacey began to giggle. "We'll beautify him,"

she said. "What do you think, Kristy? We do have a tub in the garage. It might be fun."

Kristy looked around the McGills' backyard, smiling. "The yard is fenced in. Everyone's in old clothes. Jenny's got her smock on. If we just tell the kids to take their shoes off. . . ."

Ten minutes later, Mallory, the four members of the Baby-sitters Club, and the ten kids had taken their shoes off and lined them up on the benches at the picnic tables. Even Jenny had consented to remove her shoes, but only after Kristy told her that Andrew would want it that way. Stacey had found the tub and told her mother what they were going to do. Now the tub was being filled by the hose while David Michael removed Louie's collar.

"What kind of soap do you use?" Stacey asked.

"Johnson's Baby Shampoo," replied David Michael.

"It makes his fur shiny and fluffy," added Kristy.

"I don't think we have any baby shampoo," said Stacey. "I'm not sure my mom will let me use up shampoo on a dog, anyway."

In the end, they used a regular bar of soap.

When the tub was filled and the soap was floating in the water, Kristy called out, "Oh, Lou-ie!"

Louie looked around, saw the tub of water, and fled to a corner of the yard.

"Oh, Lou-ie!" cried David Michael.

"Oh, Lou-ie!" cried most of the rest of the kids.

David Michael, Buddy, and Charlotte began stalking Louie around the yard.

"You shouldn't have taken his collar off so soon," Charlotte pointed out.

"I know," said David Michael, "but we'll get him,"

And they did. The three of them ambushed him from behind a fir tree. Then they surrounded him, joined by Suzi and Margo, and hustled him over to the tub.

"Okay, in you go, boy," said Kristy. She and David Michael heaved him into the water. They looked as if they were used to doing so.

SP-LASH! A sort of tidal wave washed over one side, soaking Jamie and Claire, who laughed delightedly.

Four kids pounced on poor Louie and began wetting him down. Nina dove for the soap and fell in the tub. After Dawn fished her out, the kids crowded around, each wanting a turn to soap Louie. During all of this, the only sound Louie made was a pitiful whine when Kristy and David Michael tossed him in the water.

When Louie was good and soapy, Mary Anne asked, "Is it time for the hose?"

"I think so," said Kristy. She helped Louie out of the tub. He stood, dripping, on the lawn, waiting for what was to come.

"He shrank!" cried Nina. "What happened? Oh, he *shrank!*"

"No, he didn't," said Dawn patiently. "He's just wet. You'll see."

Mary Anne approached with the hose.

"Shouldn't someone hold him?" asked Dawn.

"Nah," said David Michael. "He knows the only way to get the soap off is to let us rinse him."

And at that moment, Louie streaked across the yard in a soapy flash. Eight children ran after him. (Jenny was cowering on a lawn chair, and little Eleanor was playing with her toes, unaware of what was going on.)

"Tackle him!" yelled Buddy.

Nicky leaped for him, but Louie slipped out of his grasp. He was running around the McGills' backyard in a big circle.

"Go that way!" cried Charlotte, pointing.

Half the kids turned around and ran in the other direction. Louie saw them coming. *He* turned around and ran into the rest of the kids.

"Gotcha!" said Margo. She, Nicky, Suzi, and Jamie fell on Louie in a slippery heap.

"Hold him!" shouted David Michael. "Here comes the water!" David Michael twisted the nozzle and a spray of water shot out. It scored a direct hit on Louie and the children.

By the time Louie was rinsed off, dried off, and calmed down, he looked beautiful. ("He's fat again," said Nina, with relief.) But the kids were soaked, and so were their clothes.

"Thank goodness it's a warm day," said Stacey. "They can dry off in the sun while they beautify Louie."

When the morning was over, Louie was a canine masterpiece. Stacey had French-braided his fur. Charlotte had tied a ribbon at the end of each braid. Margo and Mallory had painted red nail polish on his claws. David Michael had run home long enough to find his plaid collar.

The children inspected him critically.

"Does he have any clothes?" asked Nicky, "A sweater or something?"

"No," said Kristy, "But I think he's dressed up enough. Now if he can just stay this way until tomorrow. . . ."

The children began to go home. David Michael was the last to leave. He led Louie proudly out of McGills' yard on the plaid leash.

It was then that Kristy turned to the other

club members. "You don't think Louie looks too much like a girl, do you?" she whispered.

Nobody said a word.

"Oh, well," Kristy went on. "If anybody asks tomorrow, I'll just say his name is Louella. They'll never know."

CHAPTER 11

Mimi's therapy really helped her. Every day she learned more things. And just like a child, she learned the physical things — like sitting up, standing up, trying to walk — pretty quickly, but her speech was coming along slowly. She reminded me a lot of Lucy Newton. Lucy could sit up, crawl, and pull herself into a standing position. She could wave bye-bye and feed herself a bottle or a cookie. But she couldn't talk.

She and Mimi were both trying hard, though. Lucy was learning to imitate sounds, and Mimi was trying to remember words. That was the funny thing about Mimi. After she was able to talk again, she sometimes mixed up her words, and often couldn't think of ones she wanted to use.

The speech therapist had given me flash cards to help Mimi's vocabulary and memory. I would hold up a picture, and Mimi would try to say the name of the object. Sometimes she would say it right away. Other times she would struggle.

Once I held up a picture of a bird. "It — it skies in the fly. No, it flies in the sky," said Mimi, sounding frustrated. "It has wings. It catches worms. It builds nests. But I . . . oh, you know what it is, my Claudia."

Other times, she would say the Japanese word for the picture instead.

I asked the doctor about it, and he said Mimi had something called aphasia. "It will get better," he assured me.

Unlike Lucy, however, Mimi had one big problem: She still had very little use of her right hand. And when she tried to walk, she limped badly on her right leg. The doctors now seemed to think that she might never get back the full use of the right side of her body, although they did think she'd get somewhat better. Just in case, however, the occupational therapist was teaching Mimi how to write and do other things left-handed.

One morning I was at the hospital with Mimi. She was sitting in an armchair and had insisted on getting dressed. We were waiting for her speech therapist to come, and I was quizzing her.

I sat cross-legged on her hospital bed. "What

color is this?" I asked, holding up a corner of the white sheet.

Mimi frowned. "*Shiroku*. . . ."

"English, Mimi. In English."

"It's . . . not black," she said finally.

"White," I reminded her.

"Oh, yes. I — I can know this." (As I said, she would mix up her words sometimes.)

I held up one of her flash cards. "What's this?"

"*Hitsuji* . . . no . . . sheep!" said Mimi.

"That's right! Hey, Mimi, you're doing great!"

"She certainly is," said a voice.

Dr. Marcus had appeared in the doorway.

I greeted him happily. I liked Dr. Marcus a lot. So did Mimi (even though she had said so in Japanese and Mom had had to translate).

"In fact, she's doing well enough to go home tomorrow."

"Home?" I cried. "Tomorrow? Oh, that's terrific!"

Mimi smiled. "Mmm," she said, nodding, and I knew she couldn't think of whatever words she wanted to use. But her smile said plenty.

That night, Mom and Dad and I held a meeting about Mimi. My parents had spent the afternoon talking to Dr. Marcus and the nurses and therapists.

"She'll have to go to the hospital every day for therapy," said Dad. "Mom and I will arrange to do that. She's supposed to be at the hospital from about two to five."

"But what will she do all morning?" I asked.

"She can look at magazines or watch TV," replied Mom. "But mostly she ought to practice what she's learning in therapy. She can't be left alone — "

"I'll stay with her," I volunteered immediately.

"You will?" asked Mom. "Are you sure? It would be wonderful if you could. We don't want to interrupt Janine's classes."

(I was sure that would be a relief to Janine. All she had done the past week was bury her nose in one book after another. She said she had exams coming up, but it seemed to me that she just didn't care much about Mimi.)

"We'll pay you, of course," Mom went on.

"Pay me!" I said. "You don't have to pay me. This is Mimi. I *want* to take care of her. I'm part of her family."

"Yes, but you'll be missing out on the play group. And you'll have to work with Mimi at least part of the time. You won't be simply keeping her company. She'll need help. It'll be a lot of work."

"We-ell . . ." I said.

"I think we ought to pay you your regular baby-sitting wages," said my father.

"I agree," said Mom.

"Okay," I gave in. "But only if you don't tell Mimi. I wouldn't want her to know I'm getting paid to help her. I think it would hurt her feelings. Deal?"

"Deal," replied my parents.

So Mimi came home from the hospital the next afternoon, and the following morning was the beginning of my first day taking care of her. Of course, I had plenty of help during breakfast, but by eight-thirty when everyone had left, Mimi and I were on our own. I knew I could call our neighbors, the Goldmans, or Stacey's mother, if we had any trouble. And all the emergency numbers in the entire country were posted by the phone in the kitchen. It felt weird, though, not to have the Thomases around for help. Kristy had moved. Her home was clear across town now.

Mimi sat in the kitchen with me while I cleaned up our breakfast dishes. Every so often I'd ask her a question.

"What am I doing now, Mimi?"

"You are . . . are . . . washing the . . . the things we eat from."

"What are those things called?"

"They are . . . plants. No, plates. And the round things we drink from."

"And what are those called?" I knew Mimi must be frustrated, but I wouldn't give up.

Questions, questions, questions. That's what the first two hours of the morning were. We walked from room to room. I asked her about everything. When she had trouble, I'd give her a memory trick to help her. (That's how my third-grade teacher helped me with my terrible spelling.)

"The next time you need to remember the name of this," I said, pointing to a chair, "picture a cherry growing bigger and bigger until is explodes, spraying out cherry juice. And when you think of *cherry*, remember the word *chair*."

"Oh, no," said Mimi, smiling. "I am sure I will call that a cherry from now on, my Claudia."

But she didn't. When I pointed to the chair about ten minutes later, Mimi frowned, then smiled. I knew she was picturing the exploding cherry. "That," said Mimi triumphantly, "is a chair."

Later, I got out Mimi's penmanship book

and she practiced writing with her left hand. When she had had a rest, she helped me make beds, doing a pretty good one-handed job.

We had just finished lunch out on the back porch, when the doorbell rang. "I'll get it!" I said. "You stay here."

I ran through the house and opened the front door. There were Stacey, Mary Anne, Kristy, and Dawn, all holding papers and packages.

"Hi, you guys!" I greeted them happily.

"Hi!" said everyone.

"We just finished the play group," added Stacey. "We thought we'd come visit Mimi."

"Oh, that's great," I said. "She's out on the back porch."

My friends followed me to the porch. When they saw Mimi, they zoomed in on her like a bunch of bees who had spotted a flower.

They all began talking at once, and dropping presents in her lap.

Immediately, Mimi forgot her words. I heard her mumble something about *kodomo*. Aside from that, she resorted to, "Mmm," and smiling. But when the girls sat down and Mimi felt less flustered, she perked up.

"I am . . . happy to see you," she said slowly.

"Oh, boy, are we ever happy to see *you*," replied Mary Anne emphatically.

"Look," said Stacey, "Charlotte made you

that flower." She pointed out what must have been the day's art project: a section of an egg carton stuck on a pipe cleaner and painted brilliant colors.

"And David Michael doesn't go to the play group anymore," said Kristy, "so he sends you a joke instead. His joke is, How many elephants can you fit in a sports car?"

"How many?" asked Mimi.

"Six. Three in front and three in back!"

"Oh. . . ." Mimi smiled, but looked mystified.

"The Thomases have moved, Mimi," I told her. "Remember? They were getting all packed up and everything."

"Oh . . . oh, yes," said Mimi, and I knew she really had remembered. "Do you like nor yew house?"

Nobody laughed. They knew what Mimi meant.

"The house is fine," said Kristy. "I'm not sure about the neighborhood, though. There aren't many kids around. Watson said most of them got sent to camp for the summer."

My friends stayed a while longer. When they left, it was time to help Mimi get ready to go to the hospital. Dad showed up at one-forty-five to drive her there, and then I had to go to the Newtons' to baby-sit.

Lucy was just getting ready for a nap when I arrived. Mrs. Newton seemed to be in a rush. "Can you finish with her?" she asked me. "I've got a meeting in fifteen minutes, and Lucy is a mess from lunch. She needs her diaper changed, too."

"Sure," I replied. "Where's Jamie?"

"On his way in. He was playing in the backyard."

"Hi-hi," said Jamie, appearing in the door-way to Lucy's room.

"Honey, I'm going to leave now," Mrs. Newton told Jamie. "You have fun with Claudia."

" 'Bye, Mommy," said Jamie casually.

Mrs. Newton dashed downstairs.

Jamie crossed the room to Lucy, who was lying on her changing table. "Hi-hi, Lucy-Goosey," he said, making a silly face at her.

Lucy smiled at him.

Jamie picked up a toy squirrel and zoomed it around Lucy while I tried to change her. Her smile became a grin, and she waved her arms in the air.

Jamie looked critically at Lucy. "Your face is messy," he said.

"I know it is," I told him. "I'm going to clean her up in a minute."

"I'll clean her up," said Jamie.

"No, I better do it," I said. "It's a big job. She's got baby food in her hair, and I need to change her undershirt, too."

"I can do it."

"Maybe," I said, "but let me do it anyway. It'll go faster."

"Boy," said Jamie crossly. Then he stood on his tiptoes and shouted into his sister's face, "Dumb baby! Why did we ever get you?"

Lucy burst into tears at the sudden noise, and Jamie stomped down the hall, muttering something about, "Won't even let me help." Then he sulked for a while. By the time Lucy woke up from her nap, though, he was his old cheerful self. He tickled Lucy and played pat-a-cake with her. And when I let him help me dress her, I thought he would burst with pride.

We had a fun afternoon, but when I left the Newtons', I was exhausted. It had been a long day. And I had the nagging feeling that Jamie and Lucy reminded me of Janine and me, but I wasn't sure why.

CHAPTER 12

Thursday

This morning I didn't baby-sit—
I Mimi-sat. Claudia was sitting
for Nina and Eleanor all day, so
Mrs. Kishi asked if I could stay
with Mimi. I was happy to, of
course, but I wasn't expecting Mimi
to be so different. She can't even
remember the simplest things
sometimes. In case any of you
stays with Mimi while she's getting
better, you should know that she
gets upset easily. Frustrated,
I guess. She yelled at me and
Mimi has never, ever yelled at me.
In fact, as far as I know, she
has never yelled at all. So be
careful.

Now, the funny thing is, although Mimi yelled at Mary Anne, she never yelled at me or Mom or Dad or Janine the entire time she was sick. Maybe it's because we're her family. I guess it's one thing for me to trail around after her, pestering her with questions, but something else for a friend of the family to do it. I bet she was embarrassed. She was probably embarrassed just for needing a sitter in the first place. After all, she was a grown woman, not a baby like Lucy Newton. Anyway, I felt terrible for Mary Anne. She's shy and sensitive, and things like this really upset her.

The reason Mary Anne was staying with Mimi was that I had told the Marshalls over a month ago that I would sit for Nina and Eleanor. Mr. and Mrs. Marshall had a very important all-day event to attend in Stamford, so they had called way in advance for a sitter. I didn't want to back out of the job, Mom and Dad didn't want to take any more time off from work than they already had, and they didn't want to ask Janine to miss a class.

So we asked Mary Anne to stay with Mimi. Of course she said yes immediately.

I didn't have to be at the Marshalls' until ten o'clock, but I told Mary Anne to come to my house at nine-thirty. That gave me plenty of time to show her Mimi's exercise book and flash cards, and to explain what things Mimi could and couldn't do, what to fix for lunch, when Dad was coming home, etc.

Mary Anne listened patiently and asked me a few questions. She knew where I'd be if she needed help. I told myself I could always bring Nina and Eleanor back to my house, if necessary.

At ten minutes to ten, I had to leave. "Okay, Mimi," I said. "I'll be over at the Marshalls'. I have to baby-sit. But Mary Anne will stay with you. Dad'll be here a little before two."

"This is fine, my Claudia," Mimi answered slowly.

I gave Mary Anne the thumbs-up sign and left.

Mary Anne said that right from the start, Mimi was, well, difficult. Not mean or anything. But, for instance, as soon as I was gone, Mary Anne suggested to Mimi, "How about working on your flash cards?"

And Mimi replied, "Oh, Mary Anne, why do we not watch the . . . the . . . big box?"

Mimi *never* watches television. Well, hardly ever. So this was pretty unusual.

But Mary Anne didn't want to argue with Mimi. She decided that maybe listening to people talking would help Mimi's speech, so she found a talk show on TV. Unfortunately, it wasn't a very interesting show. It was about tax reform or something. Mary Anne was bored immediately, and after about five minutes, she realized that Mimi wasn't even looking at the screen.

Mary Anne jumped up, flicked off the TV, and said, "Come on, Mimi. It's a beautiful day. Let's sit on the porch and I'll help you with your flash cards."

Mimi heaved a big sigh, but apparently couldn't think of anything to say. She let Mary Anne help her out to the porch.

When they were settled, Mary Anne held up the top card.

"Kitchen," said Mimi.

"No, *chicken*, " Mary Anne told her.

Mimi remained silent.

"Say *chicken*," Mary Anne prompted her.

"Chicken," whispered Mimi.

I could just picture the two of them on the porch with the flash cards. Mary Anne was wearing a jeans skirt, a pink and white striped blouse, and loafers with no socks. I'm sure she was perched on the edge of her chair with her feet crossed. One hand was probably holding up the cards, and the other was probably playing with her hair.

Mimi would have been sitting just as primly

in her chair, only settled well back in it, since her balance wasn't very good. She had put on a blue pants suit that morning, and I had helped her choose a little gold peacock to pin on her blouse. Lately, she had taken to sitting stiffly and sort of cradling her useless right arm in her good left one.

Mary Anne held up the next card.

Mimi looked thoughtful. Then her face grew pink. *"Hitsuji?"* she suggested after a moment. "No . . . no. . . ."

"It's a sheep, Mimi," said Mary Anne.

"Ah. Mmm. . . ." Mimi's speech was disappearing, along with her nerve.

"Say it," said Mary Anne.

This may have been the real beginning of the problem. I'm not sure. The thing about Mary Anne is that although she's shy, she can sound sort of schoolteacherish sometimes. In fact, she said recently that she wants to be a teacher one day. Maybe Mimi thought Mary Anne was being pushy, or treating her like a child. ("Say da-da, Lucy. Say da-da. Oh, what a good girl!")

"Say it," Mary Anne said again.

"Sheet."

"No, sheep. *Puh, puh.*" Mary Anne emphasized the p-sound at the end of the word, which I'm sure Mimi had heard just fine and had meant to say. It just hadn't come out right.

"*Sheep.* PUH. PUH," Mimi repeated loudly.

Mary Anne hesitated then. She wondered if she should forget about the cards, but she remembered my saying that if Mimi wanted to get better, she would have to drill, drill, drill every day. Even Saturday and Sunday.

So Mary Anne held up the next card. It showed a baseball bat — for some reason, one of the toughest words for Mimi to remember.

"Mmm," said Mimi. "Mmm. . . ."

"No," said Mary Anne. "Buh, buh."

"Buh . . . buh . . . be *quiet!*" said Mimi as loudly as she could. She got unsteadily to her feet. "Be *quiet!*" she shouted again. She started to teeter off the porch into the house.

Mary Anne stood up nervously.

"And leave alone! I can do myself!" said Mimi.

"All right. All right. I'm just coming along behind you. I won't help you," said Mary Anne. She followed Mimi. What, she wondered, should she do if Mimi locked herself in her bedroom?

But Mimi made her way into the kitchen, holding onto her right arm the whole way, even though Mom and I had told her many

117

times to use the cane she'd been given by her physical therapist.

In the kitchen, Mimi sat down huffily for a few moments. Then she stood up again and began slamming the cupboard doors.

"Mimi?" asked Mary Anne. "What — "

"Special tea," Mimi managed to say. "We need it."

"Oh," said Mary Anne, relieved. "You're right. We do. How about, um, how about. . . ." (Poor Mary Anne was so nervous about upsetting Mimi that she hardly knew what to say.) "I could get out the special cups and the pot, if you'll find the tea."

"Yes, yes." Mimi began to calm down.

Twenty minutes later, the tea was before them. Mary Anne had made it (following Mimi's garbled instructions), but Mimi was able to pour left-handed.

She and Mary Anne each took a sip.

"Ah," said Mimi. "Good."

"Wonderful," agreed Mary Anne. "We haven't had special tea in a long time."

"Mary," said Mimi, "I am sorry. I did not mean to . . . talk at you."

"That's okay," said Mary Anne. "I think I deserved it."

"No one deserves rude." Mimi put down

her cup and held out her left hand. Mary Anne took it. Mimi smiled at her. "All forgive?"

"Yes," said Mary Anne. "And I have a suggestion. Let's play hooky."

"Hooky? Oh . . . yes!" Mimi laughed.

Mary Anne laughed, too.

They spent the rest of the morning watching game shows on TV. Mimi got pretty good at *Wheel of Fortune*. I decided that she should watch it every morning.

CHAPTER 13

On the day before Lucy Newton's christening, I worked with Mimi in the morning, as usual. She and I had never discussed her blowup at Mary Anne, and Mimi had been quite cooperative with me, my parents, and her therapists since then. We could see improvement every day. Her speech was getting better and her limp was going away. She still didn't have much use of her right arm, though, and the occupational therapist worked hard with her to increase the use of her left hand. That was difficult for Mimi, since she used her hands a lot — cooking, embroidering, knitting, sewing. And no matter how well she learned to use her left hand, there were some things she'd never be able to do one-handed. I found her bag of knitting needles stashed in the hall closet one day.

Mimi was sad and disappointed, but she wouldn't complain.

After Dad came to take Mimi to the hospital that day, I went to the Newtons' house. Mrs. Newton was in a panic. Jamie had a cold and Lucy was cutting a tooth. Both of them were crying.

The dining room was a shambles. Mrs. Newton had set out every plate, dish, and piece of silverware she planned to use at the party the next afternoon. And by each dish and bowl was the food that was going to go on it or in it. There were packages of decorations, stacks of plates for the guests, and boxes of cocktail napkins and matches that said Lucille Jane Newton and the date of the christening on them in silver letters. And there were little notes on yellow paper stuck everywhere. They said things like: *Remember carrot sticks in fridge*, *Don't forget to salt*, and one I didn't understand at all that was stuck to an empty jar and read, *Auntie Nora's swizzle sticks.*

Mrs. Newton looked as much a wreck as the dining room. She was wringing her hands and surveying the room warily, as if it were going to crumble away at any moment.

"Oh, Lord, what if it *rains?*" she exclaimed. "We'll have to hold this thing in*side.*"

"Well, the Baby-sitters Club will be there to help you," I reminded her. My friends and I had been invited to the christening and the party as "paid guests." We were going to keep an eye on Jamie and Lucy, and help Mr. and Mrs. Newton pass food, fill trays, make ice cubes, and do other party stuff.

"Claudia, how would you like to decorate the yard tomorrow?" Mrs. Newton asked me. "That is, if it doesn't rain. You're so good at things like that."

"I'd love to," I told her. "When should I come?"

"Let's see. The service will be at two. Why don't you come over around noon? You could help get the children dressed afterward." Mrs. Newton glanced at the sniffling, tear-stained Jamie and Lucy. "Oh, I hope they're better by then," she added.

"By head hurts," wailed Jamie.

"Wahhh . . ." added Lucy pitifully.

Mrs. Newton looked pained, but she turned the children over to me and got to work. While she bustled around with her party things, I rubbed teething medicine on Lucy's gums, handed tissues to Jamie, and tried to keep both of them happy and quiet by reading them picture books. Jamie's current favorite story was *The Saggy Baggy Elephant*, and we read that one six times.

When it was time for me to leave, Jamie smiled and said he felt a lot better. Only he didn't sound any better. What he had said was, "Thacks, Claudy. By head does't hurt iddy-bore. I feel buch better."

"Keep your fingers crossed," Mrs. Newton said as I started down the front steps.

"Oh, I will," I told her. "All of them. My toes, too."

Of course, I didn't really keep all my fingers and toes crossed. But as I was getting dressed for the christening the next morning, I crossed two of my fingers briefly, and hoped for good weather and healthy kids.

I chose a new outfit, one I liked a lot. It was a big, loose white shirt with black splotches all over it, and white pants that came to just below my knees. My shoes (and I might point out that I'd had a fight with Mom over permission to buy them) were dainty gold sandals that laced partway up my legs. Then I put on my pink flamingo earrings and a pink bracelet that said CLAUDIA in heart-shaped beads. Finally, I braided my hair into four long braids, tied a ribbon around the top of each, and fastened the ends with butterfly clips.

I was all ready. I wasn't wearing a very churchy outfit, but after all, it was Saturday and we weren't going to an actual church service — just to a ceremony in a church.

A little while later I found myself in the Newtons' backyard, surrounded by balloons, lanterns, and miles of crepe paper. I hung everything as artfully as I could. Then I asked Mr. Newton if there happened to be a couple of strings of Christmas lights handy. Surprisingly, there were. I arranged the strings on some bushes by the back porch and plugged them in. The twinkling gold lights made the yard look festive.

I called the Newtons outside.

"It's lovely!" exclaimed Mrs. Newton.

"You did a fine job, Claudia," added Mr. Newton.

"Is this all for Lucy?" asked Jamie, who had miraculously recovered from his head cold.

"Well, it's all for Lucy's party," his father told him.

"I thought so," said Jamie. He disappeared indoors.

"Oh, dear," said Mrs. Newton, "I think we've got a problem. The children are well, but Jamie's suffering from jealousy."

"I'll start getting him dressed," I said. "It's almost one o'clock. Kristy and the others will be here in half an hour."

I found Jamie in his room, sitting sulkily on his bed.

"Time to get dressed," I said cheerfully.

"For the party?" asked Jamie.

"Yup."

"Nope."

"What do you mean, nope?"

"I'm not getting dressed."

"Yes, you are. Look." I held out the new clothes Mrs. Newton had bought him — a very preppy little outfit: khaki slacks, a white button-down shirt, a navy blazer, and topsiders. "See how grown-up you'll be? Just like Daddy."

Jamie hesitated. "All right," he said grumpily after a few moments.

He let me help him with the buttons and laces. When we were finished, I gasped. Jamie didn't look like the little Jamie Newton I knew. He looked like a real boy. Shocked, I led him to the kitchen where Mr. and Mrs. Newton were doing last-minute food things. They must have been more used to him than I was, because all they said was how nice he looked and how well his blazer fit.

"Shall I dress Lucy now?" I asked.

"I'll do it, thanks," replied Mrs. Newton, "but come give me a hand. I can't wait for you to see her dress."

When Lucy was dressed she didn't look any older or younger than usual, but she did look like an angel. Her christening outfit was a long white gown with lots of lace and ribbons, tiny pearl buttons on the back, and a matching cap. We finished dressing her just as Kristy, Mary Anne, Stacey, and Dawn showed up.

There was plenty of oohing and aahing, and I think every one of them said at least once, "Isn't she *cute?*"

Lucy smiled at us from under her cap, and Jamie glared at us darkly.

Trouble was brewing.

The christening ceremony at the church went by quickly. The guests and we baby-sitters sat in the first few rows of pews, while the Newtons stood at the front of the church with the minister and the man and woman who were going to be Lucy's godparents.

Lucy let out a little cry when the minister touched her forehead with the water, and Jamie kept leaning over to examine his new shoes, but otherwise things went well. Unless you count the very end of the ceremony, when the Newtons were walking down the aisle toward the back of the church, and Jamie turned around and called over his shoulder to the minister, "Hey, God bless you!"

Everyone laughed, but it didn't matter, because the christening was over and it was time to go to the Newtons' for the party. The members of the Baby-sitters Club got ready to switch from being guests to being helpers.

Mr. Newton drove us from the church to the party. Mrs. Newton put us to work right away. Kristy and Stacey were to pass out hors d'oeuvres, Mary Anne and Dawn were to help set up the food table, and I was to watch Jamie.

Lucy apparently wasn't going to need much watching. She was the center of attention, passed adoringly from one pair of arms to the next.

Jamie was torn between watching all that, and not watching it. When he wasn't watching, he tried to perform daredevil tricks on his jungle gym.

"Hey, Gram! Look at me!"

But usually Gram (or Gramps or Auntie Nora or whomever he was calling) was too enthralled with Lucy to pay much attention to him.

"Roarrrr!" shouted Jamie, standing at the top of his slide and beating his chest. "I'm King Corn!"

The only attention that stunt attracted was from his mother. "Honey, not so loud, please."

"Anyway," I whispered to him as I helped him off the slide, "it's King *Kong*, not King Corn."

"Oh."

When the food had been eaten and the guests were happily stuffed, Kristy and the others helped clear the table. Then they began to pile it up with the gifts the guests had brought.

"Presents!" yelped Jamie eagerly. "Maybe they're for me!"

"I . . . I don't think so," I told him.

"Why not, Claudy? Who're they for?"

"Well, I think they're for Lucy. For her christening."

"All of them?"

"Probably."

"Are you sure?"

Jamie just couldn't believe that the entire stack of presents before him was for Lucy. And, in fact, he was right; not all of them were for Lucy. There were a few small things for him: some Match Box cars and a tiny teddy. But the majority of the heap was dresses and stuffed animals and toys for Lucy.

Jamie made his unhappiness plain. "Leave me alone," he told me crossly.

I knew how he felt, so I did leave him alone. The party was sort of coming to an end, anyway. I joined my friends, who were looking at the Polaroid pictures Mr. Newton was taking. It was fun to watch each print change from a brownish blank to a clear color photo.

I'm not sure what made me look up to see who was holding Lucy at the moment, but I did — and I couldn't see anyone holding her. So I scanned the yard and saw that she'd been placed in her bouncy walker chair. She was sitting by one end of the food table, next to a half-empty pitcher of fruit punch that had been left out. As I watched, Jamie spotted both Lucy and the punch. He darted toward her, lifted the pitcher, and —

I ran across the yard as fast as I could, knowing I'd never reach them in time. I could just picture Lucy's beautiful gown all stained with red punch.

"Jamie!" I shouted. "No!"

But before the words had actually left my mouth, Jamie was putting the pitcher back on the table. And by the time I got to him, he was tickling Lucy's bare feet.

"Jamie," I gasped, "I thought you were going to pour that punch on your sister."

Jamie looked at me guiltily. "I was," he said, "but I changed my mind."

"How come?" I asked.

Jamie shrugged, then frowned. "'Cause I love her," he said at last. "She *is* my sister."

Hmm, I thought, remembering when I'd raised my hand to hit Janine, but had stopped just in time.

The party ended a little while later. Jamie's words didn't come back to me until I was on my way home. Then I began to think about Janine. Janine was my sister and I was hers. I supposed we loved each other, although we'd never actually said so. I hadn't thought much about it. Mostly what I thought about was how much attention Janine got from everybody. Janine was such a brilliant student. Janine was going to be a physicist. Don't interrupt Janine, she has to study. Janine this, Janine that.

It was kind of the way Jamie probably felt about Lucy. Lucy was so pretty. Lucy did such adorable things. Be quiet, Lucy's asleep. Lucy this, Lucy that.

And yet — I knew that Lucy wasn't more special to anyone than Jamie was. Did that mean that I was as special as Janine? And underneath, did I really love Janine the way Jamie said he loved Lucy? *And*, if *I* loved Janine, did *she* love the rest of us back — but just didn't know how to show it?

I wasn't sure at all.

I struggled through our front door after the party that afternoon. My arms were loaded with things. Mrs. Newton had sent my friends and me home with leftover party stuff. I had a stack of Lucy napkins, a container of pastries, some cookies, some peanuts, and half a bag of M&M's.

"Hello!" I called.

"My Claudia?" came a tentative voice from the back porch.

"Hi, Mimi!" I ran to her, and showed her the things from the party. "They had special napkins and matchbooks made," I told her. "Here. Do you want to try a pastry? They're really good."

Mimi took one and began eating it neatly, using her left hand.

"Hey," I said suddenly, "where is every-one?" Mimi wasn't supposed to be left alone.

"Your parents had to . . . to leave," Mimi replied carefully. "Janine is here."

"Where?" I asked.

"Room."

"She's in her room? Is she working?"

"Think so."

"Are you all right down here for a while?"

"Yes. Surely."

I ran upstairs, pounded on Janine's door, then let myself in without waiting for her to answer.

"Claudia!" she said, frowning. "Is something the matter?" She was in front of her computer, as usual. I was surprised her face hadn't turned green from the glow yet.

"Mimi is downstairs all by herself. She's not supposed to be alone."

"I've been right here," said Janine uncomfortably.

"You're supposed to be *with* her," I pointed out. "Can't you do *any*thing for this family? Is it too much to ask that you spend an hour with our grandmother?"

Janine dropped her hands into her lap. "I just couldn't," she mumbled. "Mimi asked me to sit with her, but I didn't know what to *do*. You're the one who's been spending so much time with her."

"You were great with her in the hospital,"

I said. "You could talk to her even when she couldn't talk back."

Janine shrugged. "Well, anyway, no one wants me as part of this family."

"What?"

"You're always pushing me into my world and out of yours."

As usual, I didn't understand what she was talking about.

Janine gave another exasperated shrug and turned back to her computer. "Go away," she said, not bothering to look at me. "Mimi prefers you to me, anyway."

"Janine, wait," I said. "I want to talk to you. Can't you turn that thing off for a minute? Whenever it's on, you look at it, not me. Besides, I think your face is turning green."

Janine gave me a hint of a smile. "All right," she said. "Just let me save this." She pressed a few keys, waited a moment, then reached around to the side of the computer and touched something or other that made the screen go blank.

I sat down on Janine's bed, and she swiveled around in her chair to face me. "What do you mean," I asked, "about pushing you into your world?"

"I mean," replied Janine, "that all I ever hear is, 'Janine, go study,' or, 'Janine, don't neglect your schoolwork.' Nobody ever asks me to accompany them somewhere or to help them — and then, more often than not, you accuse me of foisting extra work onto your shoulders."

"But you do!" I exclaimed. "You sit around in your room with your books while I have to cook, go to the hospital, work with Mimi. . . ."

"Recall, if you will," said Janine, "what happened when Mom and Dad made the decision to rearrange our schedules — "

"Our lives," I interrupted.

" — in order to work with Mimi."

"I got stuck with the mornings and had to drop out of the play group, while you got off scot-free," I said.

"No," Janine went on. "Let me refresh your memory. I started to speak and you rushed into the conversation, *volunteering* your mornings. Mom then thought that was such a wonderful arrangement that I had to pretend I wouldn't have been able to help Mimi in the first place. And what about the day Mary Anne was asked to attend to Mimi? No one told me that was to happen. If someone had mentioned it, I could have arranged to miss a class. But no one thought to inform me. It's as if I don't exist."

"Well — "

"How about those times you blamed me for not helping you with dinner? Did I realize that task had fallen to you? No."

"But — "

"I am many things, Claudia, but I am not psychic. I do not have ESP."

"But Janine," I said. "You're everyone's favorite. You're so smart — "

"*I'm* everyone's favorite!" she cried. "No, *you* are. You're popular and pretty — "

She stopped. We smiled at each other.

"Look," I said, "maybe we haven't been good about including you in things, but this business is not all our fault. It's — it's a two-way street," I said, quoting my father. "Maybe we wouldn't have been so quick to put your studies first if you hadn't always made us feel that your work was so important to you."

"It *is* important to me," said Janine. "But not more important than my family."

"You know what?" I said slowly. "I think you ought to talk to Mom and Dad. I think you should tell them this. Mimi, too. I bet they don't have any idea how you feel."

Janine turned her head away. "I don't know. . . ."

"And if you can't talk to them," I said, "then show them."

"How?"

"Start spending some time outside of your room. Do you really have to study nonstop?"

"No."

"Then spend some time with us. The next time Mimi wants company drill her on her flash cards. Or help her learn to use the special equipment the therapist gave her to teach her to do things one-handed. Or just talk to her.

"Or some evening when it's about six o'clock," I went on, "go down to the kitchen and see if someone needs help with dinner. It's like . . . I don't know. Maybe if you change, Mom and Dad and Mimi and I will change, too."

Janine nodded her head. "I see," she said. "Yes. That's very sensible. . . ."

"But don't change too much," I added. "Mom and Dad'll die if they don't get a physicist out of this family."

Janine laughed.

I stood up.

"I'll tell you something," said Janine. "For a little sister, you're pretty smart."

"Moi?" I said, grinning.

"Toi," Janine replied with a smile. It was the closest she'd come to making a real joke in a long time.

Janine stood up, too. "I wonder . . ." she started to say.

"What?" I asked.

"I wonder if it's too late in the day for special tea with Mimi. Let's see. Mom and Dad will be out for a while. . . . No, I don't believe it's too late."

"Not if you start right now," I said encouragingly.

Janine straightened up her desk. Then I followed her out of her room, but I let her go downstairs alone while I went to my own room. A half hour later I crept down to the kitchen. There were Mimi and Janine, sitting across the table from each other. They were drinking tea from Mimi's cups, and were involved in a conversation about being left-handed versus being right-handed. Truthfully, the conversation sounded a little dull. But Mimi's eyes were sparkling, so I knew she was very, very happy.

CHAPTER 15

July was over. The play group was over. Summer vacation was half over. A new family had moved into Kristy's house. And Mimi was still improving. It was a different sort of summer — a summer of change.

I remarked on that to Mimi one hot, damp afternoon as we sat on the porch, trying to keep cool. Mimi was fanning herself with a delicate Japanese fan that she could open and close expertly with her left hand. I was aiming a tiny battery-operated fan directly at my face and neck, which were hotter than the rest of me, since my hair clung stickily to them. I couldn't find a good place to rest the fan, so I just held it and moved it slowly around.

"Time is change," Mimi told me importantly. I frowned. "I don't understand."

"As long as there is time, there is change."

"You mean things are always changing?"

Mimi nodded.

"Sometimes they seem to change faster than other times," I said. "I mean, look at everything that happened just this month. We had a play group. Kristy moved out. That new family moved in — the Perkinses. You got sick, and then you got better. . . ."

"Have you met these Perkinses?" asked Mimi.

But suddenly I found that I couldn't answer her. Over and over I heard myself say, "You got sick, you got sick." A huge lump was building up in my throat. I turned my fan off and set it down.

"Mimi, I'm sorry," I whispered, unable to look at her.

"Sorry? For what?" Mimi became very concerned. She snapped her fan closed and leaned toward me. "What is it, my Claudia? What is wrong?"

"I gave you the stroke, didn't I? I was rude to you that night, and then you went to your room and the next thing I knew, you had fallen on the floor."

"Oh, my Claudia," murmured Mimi. "Is that what you think?"

I nodded miserably. "It's the truth, isn't it?"

"No. It is not the truth. I had not been feeling well for a long time. Very tired. Did you not notice?"

I thought hard. "I guess so."

"Look at me, my Claudia. This is an old baby, I mean, body. It is winding down. All parts have been working hard for many, many years. So, one of them wore out. That is all."

I tried to smile.

"Do you believe me?" asked Mimi.

"I want to."

"I can't make you believe me, but I will tell you again. What I said is the true . . . the truth."

"Honest?"

"Yes. Honest."

I turned my fan back on, feeling lighter. I was just about to ask Mimi if we could use her tea things to make special iced tea, when we heard a car door slam in front of our house. A few moments later, Janine appeared.

"Hi," she greeted me. She crossed the porch and gave Mimi a kiss on the cheek. "Hello, Mimi. How are you?"

"Fine, thank you," replied Mimi, even though I knew she was as uncomfortably hot as I was.

"I'm starved," said Janine. "I didn't get to eat lunch today. As soon as I have a snack, would you like to take a walk, Mimi?"

"A walk?" Mimi and I repeated at the same time. Mimi had rarely left the house since she'd come home from the hospital, except of course to go back to the hospital for therapy.

"We'll walk down the shady side of the street," said Janine.

"Well . . ." began Mimi.

I thought about it. With her cane, Mimi was pretty steady on her feet. Her physical therapist had told her that light exercise would help. I didn't see why she couldn't go outside, as long as someone was with her. And it was *very* nice of Janine to make the offer.

"I think it's a great idea," I told Mimi. "Wouldn't you like to take a walk? Janine will be with you."

"All right," said Mimi slowly. Then she began to smile. "A nice idea."

I stood at the front door a while later, watching Janine and Mimi cross the front lawn, arm in arm. "Time is change," Mimi had said. The more I thought about it, the truer it seemed. It was a smart thought from a smart woman. I remembered how, not long ago, I had compared Mimi to Lucy Newton. How could I have done that? Mimi wasn't like a baby. At least not anymore. She was my grandmother, and I was glad to have her back.

"Club notebook?"

"Check."

"Club record book?"

"Check."

"Treasury?"

"Check."

"M&M's?"

"Check."

We giggled. The members of the Baby-sitters Club were gathered in my room, preparing for a meeting. Kristy, taking charge, was seeing that we were prepared.

I passed around the M&M's, proudly wearing my newest pair of earrings. They were green, shaped like bottles, and said COCA-COLA on them.

Everyone crowded around for a look.

"Okay," said Kristy after a moment. "Down to business."

But before she could say another word, the phone rang.

"I'll get it," I said, reaching for the receiver. "Hello. Baby-sitters Club. . . . Yes? . . . Yes? . . . Oh, sure. I just need a little information first."

When I hung up a few minutes later, everyone was looking at me eagerly. They knew we had new clients. "Well?" asked Kristy.

"It's the people across the street in your old house," I said.

"Mr. Perkins?"

"Well, it was his wife calling. She read the flier we left in the mailbox, and she needs a sitter on Saturday afternoon. There are two little girls. Myriah is five-and-a-half, and Gabbie is two-and-a-half. I've got all the details."

Mary Anne checked the calendar in our record book. Kristy ended up with the job for the new clients.

"Lucky!" I said. "We'll be dying to hear. Mrs. Perkins sounds really nice."

Ring, ring.

"I'll get it this time," said Dawn, diving across me. "Hello. Baby-sitters Club. . . . Hi, Mrs. Pike. . . . *Really?* You're kidding! . . . For two *weeks?* . . . When? . . . Oh." (Dawn's "oh" sounded very disappointed.) "Well, I'm sure someone — What? *Two* someones? Okay. We'll have to do some checking. Permission and stuff. We might not be able to get back to you until tonight. . . . You would? Yeah, that'd probably make a big difference. Okay. And *thanks.* 'Bye."

"What, what, *what?*" cried Kristy, even before Dawn had put the receiver back in its cradle.

"You will *never* guess," said Dawn.

"So *tell.*" Kristy's eyes were bugging right out of their sockets.

"The Pikes are going on vacation this month. Two weeks in — "

"Sea City. We know," said Kristy. "The beach in New Jersey. They go every summer."

"Well, *this* summer," said Dawn, "Mr. and Mrs. Pike want some time to themselves, so they're looking for two mother's helpers to come along on the vacation. Two of *us*."

"Aughh!" Everyone began squealing and jumping around.

"*Which* two of us?" asked Kristy, suddenly sober.

"Any two. Mrs. Pike said she'll be happy to talk to our parents. But I can't go," said Dawn. "I'm spending the first two weeks of August in California with my dad. Remember?"

"And we're going on vacation," I reminded my friends. "The doctor said Mimi is well enough."

"Well, I'm positive Mom won't let me go," said Kristy. "She wants all us kids around for the rest of the summer. We had a family meeting about it just last night. She says we have a big job ahead of us: learning to get along as a family. She even wants Karen and Andrew to spend extra time at Watson's — I mean, at our house — so we can really see what our new family is like."

"Well," said Stacey, "that leaves you and

me, Mary Anne. I haven't got any plans. How about you?"

"Me, neither," replied Mary Anne.

"It won't be easy to convince my parents to let me go," said Stacey.

"Or to convince my father," added Mary Anne.

"But I have this funny feeling," Stacey went on, "that pretty soon you and I are going to be getting ready for surf, sun, and fun!"

"Yeah!" said Mary Anne enthusiastically. "Sea City, here we come!"

About the Author

ANN M. MARTIN grew up in Princeton, New Jersey, and was graduated from Smith College. She has written many books for young readers, among them *Bummer Summer, Inside Out, Stage Fright, Me and Katie (the Pest)*, as well as the other books in the BABY-SITTERS CLUB series (all of which are available in Apple Paperback editions).

Ann Martin lives in New York City with a cat named Mouse.

Form Your Own

BABY-SITTERS CLUB!™

ɔu and your friends can form your own chapter of The Baby-
tters Club with your official Baby-Sitters Club Kit! Here's how:

Write down your favorite baby-sitting tip. How do you make
ɔur job easier? Handle emergencies? Quiet crying babies?
et kids to go to bed on time? **OR...**

Tell us about your funniest baby-sitting experience. The
eirdest family you ever sat for...the scariest thing that ever
appened while you were sitting...the strangest kid...the most
diculous "baby-sitting disaster!"

Send us your tip or story, plus $1.95 to cover shipping
d handling. We'll send you a Membership Charter, Parent
nergency Info Sheets, and more...PLUS, we'll choose the
st tips and stories for The Baby-Sitters Club Newsletter, also
:luded!

nd check or money order (no cash please), and your tip or
ɔry (write your name, address and age on each page) to:

> The Baby-Sitters Club
> Scholastic Books
> Promotion Dept., 10th floor
> 730 Broadway
> New York, NY 10003

fer good while supply lasts.

Bring home
SLEEPOVER FRIENDS!

Here's an exciting excerpt from *PATTI'S LUCK #1,* coming in August:

Patti arranged her hair into a row of purple spikes, sort of like the Statue of Liberty's crown. Stephanie's purple curls stuck straight out, as though she'd had an electric shock.

Kate was reading the label on the jar of styling gel. "This stuff stains cloth," she said. "We'd better wash it out before it gets on anything."

Patti went into the bathroom. But she was out in a second.

"No hot water? Let it run for a minute or two," Stephanie told her.

Patti shook her purple head. "No," she said. "There's *no water at all.*"

The water main hadn't been repaired when we started home the next morning. Our purple hair was standing straight up.

Donald Foster was in his front yard, fiddling with a lawn mower. "Looking good, girls! Where are your broomsticks?"

Broomsticks, bad luck, witches.... After all that happened at the sleepover, I couldn't help thinking of ... the *Beekman curse.* What if Kate's words were right, and the time was right, and the moon and the stars were in the right places?

Truth or dare, scary movies, all-night boy talk—they're all part of SLEEPOVER FRIENDS.

Watch for back-of-the-book information on how *you* can get the official SLEEPOVER FRIENDS Sleepover Kit—everything you need to know to have a great sleepover party!

Coming in August... **PATTI'S LUCK Sleepover Friends #1** by Susan Saunders $2.50/$3.50 Can.

📖 Scholastic Books

Delicious New Apples®

Exciting Series for You!

ANIMAL INN™ by Virginia Vail

When 13-year-old Val Taylor comes home from school, she spends her afternoons with a menagerie of horses, dogs, and cats—the residents of Animal Inn, her dad's veterinary clinic.

PETS ARE FOR KEEPS #1	**$2.50 / $3.50 Can.**
A KID'S BEST FRIEND #2	**$2.50 / $3.50 Can.**
MONKEY BUSINESS #3	**$2.50 / $3.50 Can.**

THE BABY-SITTERS CLUB™ by Ann M. Martin

Meet Kristy, Claudia, Mary Anne, and Stacey...the four members of the Baby-sitters Club! They're 7th graders who get involved in all kinds of adventures—with school, boys, and, of course, baby-sitting!

FREE
Baby-sitters Kit!
Details in Books 1, 2, and 3

KRISTY'S GREAT IDEA #1	**$2.50 / $3.50 Can.**
CLAUDIA AND THE PHANTOM PHONE CALLS #2	**$2.50 / $3.50 Can.**
THE TRUTH ABOUT STACEY #3	**$2.50 / $3.50 Can.**
MARY ANNE SAVES THE DAY #4	**$2.50 / $3.50 Can.**

APPLE® CLASSICS

Kids everywhere have loved these stories for a long time...and so will you!

THE CALL OF THE WILD by Jack London
After being stolen from his home, Buck—part St. Bernard, part German Shepherd—returns to the wild...as the leader of a wolf pack! **$2.50 / $3.95 Can.**

LITTLE WOMEN by Louisa May Alcott (abridged)
The March sisters were more than just sisters—they were friends! You'll never forget Meg, Jo, Beth, and Amy. **$2.50 / $3.95 Can.**

WHITE FANG by Jack London
White Fang—half dog, half wolf—is captured by the Indians, tortured by a cowardly man, and he becomes a fierce, deadly fighter. Will he ever find a loving master?
$2.50 / $3.50 Can.

Look in your bookstores now for these great titles!

📖 **Scholastic Books**

APP871